REMEMBERED ANGER

by Martha Albrand

Black Gat Books • Eureka California

REMEMBERED ANGER

Published by Black Gat Books
A division of Stark House Press
1315 H Street
Eureka, CA 95501, USA
griffinskye3@sbcglobal.net
www.starkhousepress.com

REMEMBERED ANGER
Originally published by Little, Brown and Company, New York,
1946, and copyright © 1945 by Curtis Publications. Reprinted
in paperback by Award Books, New York, 1957.

ISBN: 979-8-88601-112-8

Cover design by Jeff Vorzimmer, ¡caliente!design, Austin, Texas
Text design by Mark Shepard, shepgraphics.com
Cover art by Lou Marchetti

First Stark House Press/Black Gat Edition: October 2024

"Martha Albrand is an expert
  at plot and suspense."
  —*Springfield Republican*

"…past grand mistress of the art
  of mystery and suspense…"
  —*American Motorist*

"Engrossing … intriguing…"
  —*New York Times*

"Danger, suspense, international
  intrigue, and hairbreadth escapes
  are the order of the day."
  —*Oakland Tribune*

"Filled with intrigue, mystery and
  romance."—*Los Angeles Reporter*

"Quickly moving, smoothly wrought."
  —*Christian Science Monitor*

1

The orchestra ceased playing abruptly. The wide room grew silent. Laughter, talk and the clatter of dishes subsided. For a second a lonely voice humming the last few notes of the popular tune could be heard. The lights hidden far above the crowd under the high ceiling flickered, darkened, then began to gleam in all rainbow colors. Red, green, blue and yellow. Then the violins joined in a sweet and gentle melody. Nothing but violins now and the lights playing, each one catching in its beam one of the four large baskets being lowered on strong silvery cords from the dome-shaped roof. The four gilded wicker baskets were filled with flowers: roses and violets and daisies; and as they swayed to the floor a girl lifted herself in each of them from among the artificial blossoms.

Applause set in, jubilant and noisy.

Chester Burton leaned back in his uncomfortable chair.

"*Un autre fine*," he told the waiter, pointing to his glass of brandy. Without realizing it he was smiling. No food, no coal, everything bearing the scars of war, yet the flower girls never failed. They and the Cancan! Without those two showpieces the old place would not be the same.

He remembered the first time he had watched them. How long ago? This was 1945.

"Nineteen forty-five," he said to himself in a low voice. Seven, almost eight years ago. On his first visit to Paris. He had been just out of college then, graduated from M.I.T. and come to France for his postgraduate work in architecture. Twenty-one, and desperately trying to look older, not quite the greenhorn he was.

There was no need any longer for him to pretend to look older than his age. The shadow of a smile wandered across his face as he thought of the embarrassment of his commanding officer, usually poker-faced and in complete control of himself, who had exclaimed upon seeing him, "Burton. Chester Burton. Impossible! I can't believe it."

It had not been surprise alone at seeing a man long since thought dead suddenly sitting opposite him which had forced the colonel to utter his amazement. After all, he had known—there had been telephone calls and messengers back and forth—whom he was to expect. It was an instinctive protest against the damage that years of suffering could do to a man's appearance—let alone to his soul.

"I thought you would find it difficult to recognize me," Chester had answered quietly. "And yet, it's because I have changed so that I am still alive. It also is the reason why I see a possibility for a job for which, to see through my way, I need your permission."

The waiter brought the brandy, adding a small round plate with the price marked on its rim on top of the other two already on his table. He was a youngish man with a sullen face and a slight limp. All of a sudden Chester felt a wild urge to crash through the other's boredom and indifference by saying casually, "*Garçon*, just for your own information, you are serving a dead man."

"You were listed as officially dead more than a year ago," his colonel had said.

Strange that this fact should have hit him so hard. Hadn't he thought of it again and again in lonely nights? Hadn't he even marked his self-manufactured calendar with the possible date when the army would cross him out of the list of missing men and pronounce him dead? Hadn't he wondered again and again if he should not reveal his true identity? Hadn't there been long hours when, afraid of what the news of his death might mean to those he loved, he had been almost ready to take the risk of asking for an interview with the German commander of the prison camp?

Officially dead more than a year ago, he thought now as he had thought a few days ago. Officially dead . . . it released Sue from all moral obligations to him and left him, Chester, with only a slight hope. Yet even this slight treasured hope he had renounced by imploring his colonel not to notify anyone that he had been found, that he was alive. It had taken hours to convince his superior officer that it would be better for him to remain dead for a little while longer, promising easier success and less danger if Chester J. Burton of Elmira, N. Y., captain in Intelligence of the American Army, remained buried in an unknown grave. No one, he thought, whom he knew would be interested in another French prisoner of war, supposedly Paul Mercier, back in Paris after three years of internment in Germany.

He looked at his watch. He had bought it only this morning. The broad leather band felt strange around his wrist. He had not been allowed to own one for more than forty months.

He was impatient for the Cancan.

And again, out of the past, came the memory of how he had sat here, almost at the very same spot, so eager to see it and then so disappointed. A bunch of ugly women, looking so old and worn out that he had been afraid they would collapse—but he had never seen such dancing.

"They're still the old guard," someone whom he couldn't remember now had said. "None of the young crop can touch them. Watch them. Just watch Josephine. The third from the right. . . ."

It was because of Josephine he had come this evening. If Josephine were still here, still alive, still dancing . . .

He had tried to get in backstage to inquire but had not been admitted then and was advised to come back later, after the Cancan.

He remembered another night, another voice.

"Josephine Vachon. Fifty-two years old! *Mon Dieu,* she is a courageous woman! Many a time I would not have known what to do without her. Get in touch with her at once, Chet. Don't go to her address. Locate her at the place she works. She is a dancer at the music hall. . . ."

So, years later, he had seen her again, doing the Cancan, tossing her black-stockinged feet into the air, kicking her head with the tip of her toes, tearing her body apart in the splits, amusing at night the Germans whom, during the day, she helped to kill.

The orchestra was playing dance music now and

the wide-open square space between the ringside tables was crowded with people. Men holding women closely, tightly, tenderly. When had he danced last? Chester Burton sighed. In another life. In a life which now seemed as sweet and unreal as a fairy tale. A life in which one was not afraid to remember, a life where a girl called Susan Porter seemed the one and only thing of importance.

"I love you, Chet! I love you so much! I know nothing will happen to you! Nothing can possibly happen to you! And, above all, don't ever forget that I will always love you!"

He reached for his brandy and gulped it down. No use thinking of it now. No use thinking of her before he had finished what he had promised himself to finish, even if it were to be the last thing he ever was able to do. Impossible, perhaps, to think of her later. Anyway, how did he know what had happened to her?

"I love you, Chet. I will always love you."

But for her he was dead. Fate had canceled her promise.

He watched absent-mindedly a thin little girl with stringy hair in a shabby dress, trying to sell small bunches of violets, obviously picked and strung together by herself. She passed him by and, with a shrug of her bony shoulders, twisted through a row of empty tables towards a corner where a few people had remained seated. He saw a man raise his hand and wave and the flower girl hastened forward. And he heard the child's voice pitched high with delight. "All of them, monsieur?"

The man answered, "All of them, *ma petite*." His

voice changed. "Didn't you tell me once you liked violets?" There was a pause, in which the flower girl moved away and the violets remained lying on the table. Then a deep warm voice answered slowly, hesitatingly, "I ... oh never mind. Don't mind me. Oh, please."

Chet could not see her clearly, half hidden as she was by a pillar, but he could hear her voice over the small distance which separated them and his hands groped vaguely into the air till they found the edge of the marble-topped table in front of which he sat. He held on to it so tightly that the blood left his knuckles and wrists.

It isn't possible, he told himself. It can't be Sue. It mustn't be Sue. I am having a hallucination just like all the others. It's because I just thought of her, because ...

"I am sorry," continued the same voice. "I think I am over it and then suddenly ... not for weeks now have I even thought of him and then tonight ..."

The voice broke and Chester could see the long sensitive hand of the man who had motioned to the flower girl move across the table and gently cover a small sunburned fist. She would always form a fist when she tried to gain control of herself. Then he heard her whispering, hardly audibly, "Don't look now, Robert, but a few tables away, back of me, sits a man. I watched him when he came in. I don't know why but somehow he reminds me of Chet. It's the way he holds his head. Chet used to ..."

People began to stream back to their tables. He couldn't understand what the man answered but a few minutes later he could hear her voice again. It said quite clearly, "Yes, of course I do, Robert."

Chester Burton sat motionless, slumped back into his chair, his hands hidden in the pockets of his trousers; only his fingers moved, playing unconsciously with a few loose French coins, which first met his palms cold as icicles, then grew warm with their perspiration.

An avalanche of emotions set loose by the unexpected sight of the woman he loved rushed through him, confusing reason and desire, impulse and reflection, his power to think clearly, his ability to move.

"I love you, Chet . . ." The same intonation . . . "Of course I do, Robert." . . . "No sir, not even my fiancée. She has suffered enough. I couldn't explain to her why I have to risk my life again and you and I know circumstances too well to kid ourselves. If I am to die now she would only have to go through it all over again." "I love you, Chet." . . . "Of course I do, Robert." . . . And, anyhow, what do I know about Susan now? Maybe she's gotten over me . . . maybe she's even married to someone else. I must not interfere. I can't come back with sudden claims after she . . . "I love you, Chet . . . I will always love you." . . . "This is dangerous business. Better that Chester Burton remain dead in an unknown grave. . . . My chances are better if . . ." But I never expected to find her in Paris. I thought she would be home in the United States. . . . What is she doing here? Where does she live? "I love you, Chet." . . . "I love you, Robert." . . . Anyhow, a crowded place is no place for us two to meet again. . . . She is not alone. . . . I must not go. . . . She must not know. Oh, for God's sake, get a hold of yourself, Chester Burton.

He took his hands out of his pockets. He reached for the empty glass and held it up. They were steady. He pulled out a package of American cigarettes and lighted one.

Out of all his confusion one fact emerged.

She had not recognized him. "Somehow he reminds me of Chet . . . the way he holds his head . . ." That his colonel had hardly believed him to be the same man who had left England one early dawn on a mission had not startled Chet. That Susan should not instantly know him shocked him beyond all reason. He sat there arguing silently with himself. How could he expect it? But if you love someone truly? Then, as a woman at the next table snapped a large compact open, he could for a second and in a flash see part of his face. What he couldn't see he knew. His hair, once chestnut brown, had turned prematurely white, the color of the old. He was wearing glasses, dark-green glasses to protect his eyes, which after years of working underground in a sulphur mine were sensitive and pained by strong clear light. His nose was crooked. A Nazi truncheon had once split the bone and without medical treatment it had set awry. A badly healed scar ran across his left cheek, pulling the corner of his lip up into his face so that now an involuntary smile had grown around his mouth. His skin was gray, not pale, not yellow, plain gray. Too long had his face and body suffered the deadly gases of the mine to be remedied by a few days of freedom. He had lost forty-five pounds and his once young strong neck was thin and wrinkled. Yes, he had changed. And she, Sue?

He moved his chair around a little so that now he could see her quite easily. The realization that even he, sitting so close to her, had not sensed her presence, that his instincts had refused to be on the alert, increased his depression.

Four years, he thought. Four years since they had seen each other. Four years of only memories. She had not changed. Not a bit. Even the dimples were still there. One, when her face was serious, right in the middle of her firm young chin, and two more when she smiled, as she did just now—one in each cheek. The short curly hair which gave her a boyish quality of gay recklessness still looked just a little bit untidy. A terrible desire to run his hand through her hair and rest it in the nape of her neck rose in him.

Sue. Sue. Sue.

Had he called her name aloud? For she turned in his direction, looking straight at him. In the next second Chester moved his head, presenting to her eyes purposely his left cheek with the scar which pulled at his mouth.

She must not know before it was all over. Then, only then, would be the time to decide how to meet her again. All emotion subsided within him, ebbing away slowly. He had come back to fulfill his task, not to wring the neck of a man called Robert.

All over the world things had changed. Men and women. Conceptions and ideas, live and dead objects. Countries had been ruined and whole cities destroyed beyond recognition. But the dressing room of this Parisian music hall had not changed. It still was no more than a narrow corridor boarded up at each end with a thin partition; just as drafty as it had been in its long and popular past. Perhaps even more so because the concussion of thunderous guns and bombs and shells had shattered many windows; and while they had been replaced out in front, no one had bothered about the back. There was little material and the prices were high. The lighting was still as poor as on that evening when Chester Burton had asked admittance under the pretense of being an ardent admirer of the dancer third from the right. Tonight he had scribbled a note. An old friend wanting to see Josephine. Two unshaded bulbs hung from the low filthy ceiling, throwing light shamelessly and indiscreetly across the dirt-littered floor and the bare walls from which plaster kept trickling every time a heavy lorry passed by or the subway rocked the building gently on its way below ground.

There was a washbasin in one corner, its enamel broken, its two taps making little noises, either because there was no water and the trapped frustrated air sighed in its metal imprisonment or because they were both dripping. Neither of them could be shut off completely. The soap dish above was grimy with dirt and loose tobacco crumbs. Even in 1937 it had never held soap.

Originally there had been mirrors across the narrow dressing table running full length along one wall, but all that remained of them now were two square pieces, one splintered by bullets.

Small cardboard cards of different colors were pinned with thumbtacks above the table, each bearing the name of the owner of that particular space. Two or three empty lunch boxes, resembling in shape and material those of butterfly drums, hung on the wall between the gaudy and incredibly dirty costumes. A large hungry cat, its back roofed high, tail standing straight, stepped stiffly away across Chester's path as he entered.

"Spit," said the Vachon. "Spit! It's bad luck otherwise." She turned to hurl a broken comb in the direction of the cat.

"I *hate* cats!" she said.

She was alone in the room. "I am sorry to have kept you waiting," she added. "Who are you?"

But she did not look at him. Instead she began to knit furiously at a sleeve of a blackish gray jumper. As she sat there on a low three-legged stool, dressed in an inconspicuous brown skirt, too narrow and too short to fit her broad muscular body, a shawl thrown over her shoulders, her hair parted straight and pinned up in a bun, she looked more like an average poor housewife than a famous Cancan dancer.

"Who are you?" she repeated.

"Sagitta," said Chet. She was one of the few who had known the code.

Vachon shrugged her shoulders. Still she did not look up.

"Don't you remember . . . ?" he urged. "Don't you remember an American called Sagitta, Josephine?"

"Never heard of you."

"I know I have changed," he said, and now he pulled

one of the low three-legged stools from under the dressing table and sat down. "I know it's hard to recognize me but the code, my handwriting alone should . . ."

"*Mon ami*," answered Josephine with unexpected authority, and now for the first time glanced up at her visitor, "I have never known Americans. Maybe a quarter of a century ago when I was young and pretty, but lately . . ." She stuck one of her knitting needles into her hair and scratched her head. "I don't like Americans," she said softly and smiled. "They are nosy and noisy . . . And what do you mean by code? I don't know any code. You mix me up. Yes, I saw your handwriting. And I swear I never saw it before. Never! I only told the night watchman to let you in because I was curious."

She leaned forward and giggled like a very young and silly girl. "An old piece like me having a visitor!" Suddenly she stared at him, her lips moving soundlessly, and Chester thought he could see her pale under the heavy make-up which apparently had not been removed for months but applied again and again, one layer over the other so that now it seemed inches deep.

"Whoever you are," she said, "they didn't treat you very nicely, did they?"

"I told you who I am," he repeated quietly, patiently. "If you don't believe me I can . . ."

"I am not interested," interrupted the Vachon. "I told you, you are mixing me up with someone else."

Suddenly Chester understood, and he smiled to himself grimly as he realized how badly he was out of training. She did not refuse to recognize him because of his changed appearance, but for reasons of her own.

"I am sorry," he said very clearly. "I am sorry, madame." And then, in a low whisper, "Is it as bad as that?"

"Worse," answered the Vachon between her teeth. "Meet me at the old place tomorrow. No, at six o'clock this morning."

As he came out of the door the night watchman gave him a big broad smile. "No luck, monsieur?"

Chester shrugged his shoulders.

"Too bad," and the night watchman slapped him familiarly on the back, "but when they are as old as Josephine they are out for the young ones."

It's my white hair, thought Chester. And just then the door behind him opened a second time and Josephine called, "Come on back, monsieur. I've changed my mind." She smiled coquettishly. "It's the privilege of women to change their minds, isn't it, monsieur?"

Chester stepped back into the tawdry dressing room.

"What made you change your mind?"

The Vachon lifted her shoulders. "Hard to tell. The cat, maybe, crossing your path. Or just because I am curious. Old women always have two vices at least. Superstition and curiosity. And then who knows what tomorrow brings? Who can tell what can happen during a night?"

Suddenly she threw both arms around him and kissed him violently and quickly. "Tell me, tell me," she whispered, "when did you come back from the grave?"

She saw the shadow of hesitation in his glance. "Don't worry, now that Emile is outside . . . it is all right. Got a cigarette?"

There was voracity in the way she inhaled the first drag and suddenly over a period of four years he could hear someone say, "And for God's sake, Chet, don't forget cigarettes for Josephine." He pulled out an almost full pack and handed it to her.

"Is there still a shortage?"

"No, but a black market." Her eyes were on him, brilliant, small pinpoint eyes. They seemed to look through all the outward changes straight into his heart. After a while she said, as if concluding a long chain of thoughts:

"Yet you're still the same." She laughed a little, hoarsely and shortly, somehow bitter. "And we thought you were dead."

"I am, officially."

For a second suspicion showed clearly in her eyes, then vanished. And as it vanished her face more and more resembled a mask.

"I came back to Paris three days ago," Chester said. "Josephine, if you only knew . . ."

"Don't tell me," she said. "Don't tell me, *cheri*."

Mixed with the tenderness in her voice was fear. Chester heard it. He had learned to detect it quickly, unerringly, in three long years of imprisonment. He looked up but she avoided his eyes.

"I don't understand," he protested. "First you seemed eager to know and now . . ."

"I made a mistake." The Vachon began to knit again, the half-smoked cigarette hanging from one corner of her mouth. "I shouldn't have called you back. I have changed my mind again. I don't want to know. I don't want to know anything."

"Why?"

Now it was contempt which showed in her face. Her answer was an angry snort. "Don't be a fool, *mon vieux*. The war is over, yes. Times have changed, but men haven't changed. Nor will they ever change. Why? Why, you ask? Because it's dangerous to know too much."

The young man with the prematurely white hair crossed his arms over his emaciated chest and regarded the stout elderly woman.

"It's true," she said defiantly. "It's dangerous to know too much."

"Then you've changed," he said finally, quietly and sadly. "You, who were never afraid. You, whom I admired for your courage. You of whom I thought in hours when I needed strength. Josephine, I thought, an old woman, a simple woman. If she can do it ... I ..."

Unexpectedly the Vachon began to cry. A few big tears slowly filled her eyes and when she no longer could hold them under her closed lids, began to roll down her cheeks, making deep dirty tracks in the make-up.

"I can't help it," she said. "I can't help it. The fire has gone out of me. A year ago I didn't care if they got me, if they tortured me, if they killed me. Now . . ." She shrugged her shoulders with a hopeless gesture. "Now . . . I am an old woman who wants to die in peace, in her own room, in her bed, an old woman who is afraid."

As if from far away they could hear the orchestra

playing dance music in the front of the building. They sat silently, both knowing that the other was thinking of the question he had put a little while ago. "Is it as bad as that?" And her answer. "Worse." It concerned the people in France, the former members of the maquis, the underground. They both had been there from the very beginning; she an active member of the maquis, he as one of the liaison officers of the Allies, chosen because of his perfect knowledge of French— the years spent studying in Paris.

Thousands had joined the maquis. But among those thousands had also been bad elements: criminals, adventurers, people eager to make a place for themselves; some of them fascists perching on the fence, unscrupulous, ambitious men. It couldn't be helped. Every man ready for any task was needed, even if he used patriotism only as a cloak to further his own ends. Some were aware of the danger in including such men and the difficulty it would present in sifting the chaff from the wheat to prevent the wrong people from achieving power.

The Vachon lifted her too-short skirt, pulled up the hem of her torn petticoat and blew her nose loudly.

"The wrong people will always get in somehow," she said. "However hard we try, we cannot help it. Well, some of them are in now. That's why it is dangerous to know too much. They use their power to kill their political enemies, street fights, accidentally. No one will ever be able to prove it. That's why I don't want to know anything. You hear me. I don't want to know anything. I am an old woman. I want to die in peace."

The fire which once had burned so fiercely in

Josephine's heart, and had spent itself till nothing but ash remained, still burned in Chester Burton. It had given him strength to endure so much, to keep on living, to come back on an early spring morning to Paris and remain officially dead.

He, more than many a man who *thought* he knew, knew the evil forces at large.

"The wrong people always get in," he repeated. "True. And among the wrong people, Josephine, there is one man, one man whom I will deal with personally. Whoever he is. Whatever he does. To find him, to expose him, I have come back . . ."

Maybe it was his voice, maybe it was his face or his white hair and the cruel scar, which made the Vachon ask, "Who?"

Chet's hands fell open in a wide, vague gesture. "I don't know," he said. "I don't know. I thought maybe you could help me."

"I," said the Vachon in a dead bored voice, all interest gone again. "I don't know anything. If I ever did I have forgotten."

"I was betrayed."

"Many have been betrayed. Many were the victims of double-crossing. Many died that way."

"I didn't," said Chet and he lifted himself from the stool and began to pace the long narrow makeshift dressing room. "I am alive only because I was determined to come back to avenge myself and all of those men who were betrayed, tortured and killed."

The Vachon said nothing.

"I was betrayed. The hour of my flight was betrayed, the place of my landing was betrayed. My mission was betrayed. They caught me the moment I hit the ground before I could untangle myself. I was in civilian clothes."

"And they tortured you," said the Vachon and began to pick nervously at her heavy eyebrows.

Chet nodded.

"Why didn't they shoot you?"

"But they did," he said quietly. "After five days of questioning they stood me up against a wall. A garden wall, big polished stones. I'll never forget that stone wall. There was a lilac bush hanging across it. A lilac bush in bloom and its smell was unbearably sweet. Yes, they stood me up with ten other men . . . only they didn't kill me. There was an air raid just as they fired. Somehow I crawled away, somehow I got over the stone wall, inside a hut. The same hut where I was to have found a man who was to help me. He lay on the floor, dead. He and a little boy. I took his papers. Or the papers I thought were his."

He stopped, swallowing hard. The lilac bush, the stone wall, the explosions of guns and bombs and lights. Death had seemed so senseless then. He could not remember having ever before in his life felt such anger as at that moment when apparently everything was over for him. He had no fear then. Maybe he would have had had they not tortured him for five days in succession. The fear of cracking, of breaking, of speaking, then the horror at seeing human beings behave as he had thought it impossible for human beings to behave, had killed his ability to be afraid. He had been past fear then. He still was.

"Go on," said the Vachon. "And then?"

"I tried to get in touch with you and couldn't. An old woman nursed me for three weeks. Then we were discovered and she was punished for harboring her 'nephew,' a man eligible for the armed services. And I was shipped to Germany."

Like a shadow the large black cat swished past them into a corner where a big rat had just come out of its hole. For a minute the rat seemed to be stronger than the cat, fighting furiously, viciously, silently, then abruptly fell dead, its neck broken by the sharp teeth of the cat.

"Wouldn't it be funny," said the Vachon staring into space, "if the rat had killed the cat?" She began to laugh hysterically.

After a while Chet said slowly, "Only two men could have betrayed me. One in London or one here in France. Who was the head of the maquis group for which you worked, Josephine?"

"I don't know," answered the Vachon and then, noticing the flash of anger in Chet's face, she sneered, "Who was your man in London? Do you know? They all had to live under assumed names, didn't they?"

"Of course," he said shortly. With an effort to control himself he added more gently, "But we knew the true identity of the man in London. He's out of the question."

"Yes," his colonel had confirmed, "excepting us only two men knew. And the one we dealt with in England and used to know as Peter Smith is Pierre Blois, who is expected to be appointed to a high office in the government. He is known as a great patriot and has distinguished himself time after time. The other, the contact man in France, Half Moon—I don't remember his real name, if I ever knew it; but I do remember that we never had any reason to distrust him. The only possibility I can see now is that an unknown third somehow managed to get hold of information."

Chet bent forward and took one of Josephine's reluctant hands into his. Stubbornly, he couldn't say why, his instinct refused to believe in an unknown third.

"Josephine," he said, "you must have known or know now who the man was who gave you orders. His code was ..."

"No!" The Vachon withdrew her hand. "I don't remember. I told you I am an old woman who's lost her memory."

She stood up suddenly and as she moved her feet made a slurring noise on the uncarpeted floor. He had not noticed that she was wearing slippers.

"My memory is very bad," she said, "but not bad enough not to remember that those you look for are members of strong groups, powerful groups, *mon vieux*, unscrupulous groups. Dangerous! I would not interfere with them. Not if I were you. You're alive. What more do you want? Why don't you go home? Why don't you go back to America? Why don't you want to live a healthy sane life? You came out of the war alive. Sane and alive. Let that be enough. Forget about revenge. Go home and be happy. You'll never succeed."

"So you refuse to help me?"

"I can't help you," she said sadly. "I would only get us both killed. You and me. Somehow. Somewhere. Why ... ?"

"It's no use," he told her. "I've made up my mind. I'll find that man even if I have to move earth and heaven, don't you understand, Josephine? Or everything I ever did and worked for and fought for would be senseless."

Suddenly the Vachon looked very tired.

"What was your name?" she asked. "The name on the note you wrote me. Mercier. Paul Mercier. That's a good common name. Be very careful not to let anyone know who you really are, Paul. And come to my house tomorrow. Around five o'clock." She found a piece of paper and a pencil in her old handbag and scribbled her address down.

"No, I cannot help you," she repeated. "But, maybe I can find someone who will help you, someone with a good memory. So many people come and go nowadays. Just like in the old times. One never knows who they are. One has to be very careful, *mon vieux*. It is not good to know too much. Good night now, and thank you for the cigarettes. And let me tell you again that you are a fool, a big silly fool."

Without looking back at her Chet left the room, pulling the door shut behind him.

He had found that very morning a small furnished room in one of the poorer side streets of the Avenue de la Grande Armée, that broad street through which Napoleon had once marched his troops on his way to conquer the world. Hitler's men had similarly marched along it towards the Arc de Triomphe; but now it lay quiet. Even the frenzied traffic which in peacetime had flooded across it in all directions no longer existed. There was still not enough gasoline to run busses or private cars and, except for military vehicles, there were only horse-drawn cabs, bicycles and pedestrians.

Chet's room was ugly, dark, facing a courtyard; and the piece of sky Chet could see was cluttered up with high, crude brick chimneys. A plaster bust of Victor Hugo occupied most of the space on a high narrow chest over which a much too large mirror hung in a heavy elaborate gilt frame. There were two upholstered chairs, imitation Louis XVI, which looked more comfortable than they were. A tiny writing desk, and an upright piano which badly needed tuning. A wardrobe which obviously once had stood in a nursery for it was painted white with big butterflies in bright colors pursuing each other, a large French double bed and hardly any space to move around in.

Yet it had seemed close to paradise to Chet when he rented it. To be able to close a door at his own will, to shut out a world which could not follow him any longer, the fantastic possession of a key, a bed only for himself, a window he could open or close whenever he felt like it, a smell which was not mixed with that of hundreds of other human beings, the whole atmosphere of safety and privacy, manifested by the unbroken bust of Victor Hugo and such a useless thing as a piano, were all like a dream come true.

As he came back into it now it was still like a dream, but he was alone in this dream. Somehow he had never thought that there might be an hour in which he would miss the enforced company of other men, an hour in which he would not have been grateful to escape the sight of others moaning, sleepless, vomiting, itching, smelling, bleeding or dying. He missed it now—being part of others, sharing the others' suffering or happiness. He was alone, cast out. Out of bounds.

Depression settled on him as he remembered his colonel's warning that he was on his own, that no one could back him or interfere. "You're on your own," the colonel had said, "you understand—strictly on your own. We cannot help you. We can't interfere in this affair. It does not concern us." And he had shrugged his shoulders. "All I can do is allow you to remain dead for a certain period, after which I expect you to report to me."

"I cannot help you," Josephine had said. "The fire has gone out of me. I am an old woman, afraid. I don't remember. I don't want to know. Do you hear? I don't want to know."

"Of course I do, Robert," Sue had whispered to another man. "I haven't even thought of him for weeks . . . somehow he reminds me of Chet."

He had become a memory to the girl he loved, an inconvenient disturbance to Josephine and a difficult case to his colonel.

All of this because one man had betrayed him. All those years because of one man. And the hundreds who had died because of his capture, of the preparations he could not make, of the interrupted contacts, the loss of time.

He threw himself on the wide soft bed, burying his face in the pillow.

"Why don't you go home to America?" Josephine's voice seemed to say. "You're alive. Let that be enough. You came back whole and sane. You are a fool."

It had been no use explaining to her what he felt; she had misunderstood him from the beginning. Had wanted to misunderstand him. Had wanted to see it all as an individual affair, a personal matter of revenge, so that she could never again be dragged into the fight.

"The war is over," she had said.

But the war against greed and selfishness and the desire for power would never stop.

He turned over and crossed his arms under his head. I wonder, he thought, how I would have felt if I hadn't sweated out those years. Maybe the war would be over for me, maybe I would go home, content to have done my duty and glad to have the job over with and forget it. Forget all about it. Forget that it was caused in the long run by all of us, by our own indifference to the things that went on around us, by our own selfishness, by our lack of feeling responsible for things which did not personally concern us.

He sat up. He said aloud as if he were still talking to the Vachon or to his colonel:

"You see, that man has become a symbol. The symbol of what we fought against. That's why I have to find him."

Suddenly he grew aware that he was speaking to himself, of his own voice ringing in the lonely room; and though he knew that he must not fall into the habit of conversing loudly with himself, he was suddenly and strangely calmed. Somehow it was good that he had been able to phrase his feelings, to put into words what this all meant to him.

"A fool?" He thought of Josephine's words and smiled.

No, he was no fool. The Vachon was a fool to give up the fight.

He began to undress slowly. On the dresser was a pile of neatly folded newspapers the former inhabitant had apparently left behind, or perhaps his landlady had put them there for a purpose. As he twisted one into two large balls to push into his shoes to keep them in shape, his glance fell on a picture and the caption running under it:

"Susan Porter from New York City, USA, who has been accredited as a correspondent for . . ." There the paper was torn and he couldn't find the end of the line. But he found the dateline on top of the page. The third of February, 1945.

And now it was May.

Three months to meet a man called Robert, three months to fall in love with him.

Carefully he went through the other papers. It took him about half an hour to find another line about her.

"Miss Susan Porter has established residence at the Hotel Atala." The Atala. For a second he closed his eyes. Very clearly he remembered the night he had told her about it.

"It's only a small hotel, Sue, in one of the side streets of the Champs-Elysées. Nothing fancy. But it has a little garden and is not expensive. Only a few blocks from the Arc de Triomphe, and, in addition to towels, long white toweling bathrobes hang in the closets. We could afford to stay there for a few weeks." They had been making plans for their honeymoon. Europe. Paris or Rome, or maybe both, and in between, Amsterdam, Bruges, Zurich.

Sue. Sue. Sue.

Very carefully, because he had no scissors, he folded the paper which carried her picture, pressing his thumbs along the edges before he tore it out and put it in his new shining wallet. Then he took it out again and looked at it. And the girl in the picture suddenly began to live, to move—was seven years old, looking exactly like a little boy, climbing over a garden fence into a piece of property which Chet owned and ruled— and when Chet, on discovering that she was only a girl, told her to scram, retorted:

"You'll be sorry. My father is the doctor around here and when you get ill I will tell him not to treat you .. . and then you'll die."

"And my father is the new minister and I will tell him to talk to God so that he won't let you enter into Paradise."

Twelve years old and proving that she had learned how to catch trout without bait and rod but in her open hands, her dirty denims rolled up knee-high, wading in the ice-cold clear water. Seventeen and dancing with him on the night of her graduation prom high school, looking strangely sweet and grown up in a white dress and kissing him for the first time.

Nineteen and a student at Vassar. No longer wanting to be a moving picture actress but a journalist, and promising to marry him on the open deck of a Fifth Avenue bus.

And Chester forgot that there was a man called Robert.

It seemed to Chet that the time was blocked, that

somehow there would never be a five o'clock. Josephine must help, he thought. I must convince her, somehow she must understand how important this is.

He sat on one of the crowded benches along the Seine. Under the gray cloudy sky the white candles of the chestnut trees looked unreal, as if a sudden flurry of snow had fallen upon their wide green leaves. A few boats were moving down under the bridges and over the railing hung old men and little boys trying to fish for food. If he turned his head towards the street at his back he could see bent figures of women and children searching the garbage cans for anything which still could be used. There were several once well-known restaurants in this neighborhood. A little further up from where he sat sprawled the buildings which housed the offices of the government.

"Times have changed," said a man next to him. He was old and crippled, wearing a crude wooden leg. Now he pointed at it. "Nearly burnt it last winter," he said. "I thought I couldn't stand the cold a minute longer but somehow couldn't quite do it. What good is a life in which one cannot even hang on to one's wooden leg?" He leaned back and sighed.

"Peace again," he went on. "One can't believe it. I remember the last peace. How Paris came back to life! All of us were dancing then. Vienna waltzes and the petite *Tonquinoise*. And, in memory of Reims and Arras, Soissons and Verdun, four terrific monuments at the Rond-Point and grandstands for hundreds of thousands on the Champs-Elysées. I saw the parade, Joffre, Foch, Pershing, Douglas Haig, the Japanese cavalry officers. Italian troops who had fought in the

Argonne, Polish and Czech troops and our 'corps' with our torn flags."

Chet smiled at him encouragingly. He remembered his father telling him about the same scene and that his mother couldn't help crying every time she thought about it. His father had been an army chaplain and had met Chet's mother during his service in France.

"And now," said the old man, "now we are dancing and singing and celebrating and maybe some are as happy as we were then but most of us are afraid. We were not afraid after the last war. At least not afraid for France. Hitler is dead and Germany finished, but they have left their traces. All over. All over the world."

A group of French officers passed slowly, then one among them in the uniform of a colonel halted his steps and another one quickly offered a match.

Chester Burton bent forward. He had seen the colonel only once in his life. For a few minutes. At midnight, shortly before he took off for his mission.

"*Bonne chance.*" the colonel had said. "Good luck, *mon capitaine*. You have your instructions. Any questions?"

There had been no questions. Only a handshake and an exchange of salutes.

No questions whatsoever. Everything had been carefully prepared. The false papers, the civilian clothes, French clothes from the Galeries LaFayette. He had been briefed by his own colonel. Everything he did not know Half Moon would tell him. Even now, sitting on a bench, watching Pierre Blois moving slowly on, he remembered that he couldn't help smiling every time those silly codes were mentioned.

His own name "Sagitta," for a star. They seemed too much part of a game invented by little boys playing cops and robbers. But it wasn't.

"There goes a hero," the old man said, "We have a lot to thank him for."

"Do you think everyone feels that way?"

The old man laughed. "Have you ever been able to generalize the French? We wouldn't be what we are if all of us ever agreed. I like him. Don't you?"

"Sure."

Somewhere a clock struck a quarter hour. Fifteen minutes past four. Chet got up. With no taxis available he couldn't tell how long it would take him to reach Josephine's address. He entered the next subway and suddenly, jolting along in a second-class compartment, was violently homesick for New York. He smiled at himself. He had thought they had managed to kill all sentimentality in him but now it seemed that in some way it only had grown stronger. The smell of the subway, the soot, the sweat, the people, the hurrying, the elbowing, women knitting, men reading their papers, soldiers flirting with girls, school children with their books in straps, the signs which forbade spitting and warnings not to open doors or windows. It all brought back Times Square, Columbus Circle, Brooklyn Bridge.

There were maps posted almost everywhere around. He studied the plan of Paris and realized he would have to change trains.

It was almost five o'clock when he reached Montmartre. Unexpectedly the sun was breaking through the clouds and for a second he could see Sacré-

Coeur brooding in sunlight. As always, groups of people were slowly climbing up the many steps which led to its portal, or coming slowly down. A flock of pigeons sailing above it all. A sudden feeling of gratitude for being alive, for being able to watch pigeons flying without anyone shooting them down as possible enemy messengers, filled Chet. He stopped at the next corner and bought a small bunch of lilies of the valley.

Josephine will help me, he thought.

The building the Vachon lived in was a three-story apartment house. He did not see a concierge as he walked through the wide, old-fashioned front door and passed the little cage of the caretaker's quarters. A row of mailboxes hung next to it. One carried Josephine's name with a little arrow pointing to the courtyard and the information, second floor left. The building stretched clear around the inner court.

As he climbed the narrow stairs he could hear a canary singing, a child crying, the clatter of a typewriter, the angry voice of a man and the growling of a dog.

Second floor left. The first door on the landing bore her name in blue chalk all across the brown wood. A radio was blaring behind it.

Chester knocked gently, then, when there came no answer, harder and finally when, except for the radio, nothing could be heard, he put his hand on the knob. The knob turned easily and as the door swung back, Chet entered the room.

"Josephine?"

He pulled the door shut behind him.

The room was empty. It was a small room with a round table under an old-fashioned hanging lamp with green pearl strings which moved gently in the current of air from a half-open window. There was only that one window and on its sill stood several little earthen pots. Chives, parsley and a plant that was dead. Three neatly tied bundles of dried chamomile hung next to it. On one wall and stuck into the frame of a cheap mirror were a dozen photographs, all of them of Josephine. A young Josephine in daring costumes with a face almost unrecognizable in its youth and beauty. Newspaper clippings, three fans, one white imitation ostrich with a tiny mirror in the center of its frame, the other two just cheap paper. And then, all by itself, in a broad red leather frame, was another picture of Josephine. In it she was sitting on a chair holding a fat sullen baby on her lap while a young man with an imposing moustache stared proudly past her into his future.

Chet smiled. Somehow he had never imagined Josephine as a mother, with a domestic life apart from the music hall. He was not worried at her not being there. In his optimistic mood he decided that she had gone personally to fetch the "somebody" who might remember that which she preferred to forget. Anyhow she must have been there shortly before; otherwise the radio would have been shut off. No average Frenchwoman would waste her money for electricity without getting something out of it.

He sat down in the chair next to the window. Into the courtyard below three people had straggled, a woman with a guitar, a man and a child. As soon as the woman began to play the man began to sing and the child took off his little cap, holding it up in the air with both hands. All around the courtyard windows flew open, heads leaned out and there was an occasional clatter of small coins hitting the cobblestoned yard, the child running for them, the man singing at the top of his lungs, "*Sous les toits de Paris*," while the woman softly and beautifully accompanied him.

Chet got up to turn off the radio and only then did he notice that there was a second door. He heard water running beyond it.

"Josephine? It's Mercier, it's . . ."

He saw her the moment he opened the door. She was hanging in the middle of the tiny kitchen.

She was hanging from a strong iron hook used usually for big smoked hams. She was dressed in a shiny raincoat which fell open across her chest and showed her nightgown, spotted and torn at the hem. Her slippers, the same worn-out slippers she had worn the night before in the dressing room, lay next to the stool which had toppled over when it was kicked away. The nails of her short small feet were polished with dark red enamel, almost perfect except for the left big toe from which it was chipped off.

The body hung from the noose of a twisted black calico kerchief, such as women wore dusting or marketing in this neighborhood. It was a carefully, expertly tied noose. The once small pinpoint brilliant eyes now popped out of their sockets and the skin had already begun to discolor.

He had seen other people hanged by their necks.

Poles and Czechs. A Frenchman who had tried to escape. He remembered the gallows in a lonely field, the tree in the prison yard, the hook in the barracks where an English boy had finished his life. He had been shocked then but this shock was greater since it was so unexpected.

"It's dangerous to know too much. I don't want to know anything. I am an old woman and afraid. An old woman who wants to die in peace, in her own bed."

Was it only yesterday that she had spoken these words?

"Josephine," he said. "Josephine."

As he moved forward he saw the note on the sink. A page torn out of a notebook, thin red lines running across it and her handwriting—yes, her handwriting.

"May God forgive me, but I cannot stand it any longer." And her name in full. Even her birth date and the little town she had been born in.

Suicide, thought Chester. Suicide. And I am responsible for it. She was afraid. Afraid to talk and afraid not to talk. She did not want to be involved in ...

In what? he thought, and again he heard her voice, that hoarse indifferent voice. "Why don't you go home and lead a healthy safe life? You came out of the war whole and sane. Let that be enough . . . They are members of powerful groups . . . I would not interfere with them."

He looked at the note again and somehow it struck him as odd that, of all persons, the Vachon should have used such trite phrasing. "I cannot stand it any longer." That was melodramatic. He read it aloud, said it over again, trying unconsciously to imitate her voice. It did not sound like her. She simply would have said, "I have had enough."

As he tried out different combinations of words he suddenly grew aware of where his suspicions led.

Murder?

Murder meant to look like suicide?

From outside, in the courtyard, still came the full-breasted singing of the man and the lovely accompaniment by the woman. And into the song Josephine seemed to repeat, "I am afraid. It's dangerous to know too much."

She had known too much.

What?

He stood motionless, his hands crossed in the small of his back, his eyes fixed at one point on the wall, as he had stood a hundred times, fighting to gain control of himself.

Then he moved cautiously forward. It wasn't the question of what she had known, and didn't want to tell him. That was of no use any longer. The immediate problem was, did she commit suicide or had she been murdered?

He went back to the entrance door and turned the key in the lock. Then, minutely, alertly, took in the room again. And he saw what he had missed before . . . the inkpot on the round table, when it should have stood on the small writing desk; the bunch of artificial flowers lying on the couch when they should have been in the cut-glass vase on the little table next to it; a wardrobe door which was half open and inside, a dress which had fallen to the floor—which might mean that someone had knocked at a moment when Josephine had already undressed for bed, and, reaching hastily for some kind of wrapper, she had picked the shiny black raincoat.

He moved back into the kitchen.

There was a glass on the sink, half filled with water. Its rim showed no trace of lipstick and Josephine had worn heavy lipstick when he saw her last. He remembered the thick layers of her makeup, the heavily painted lips.

He went back into the room. In spite of the inkpot and the flowers, it still looked too tidy. Just a bit too tidy for the Vachon. Something glittered and Chet bent down and picked up one of her long knitting needles. Then he saw the jumper on which she had knitted so furiously in her dressing room lying on a chair. Both needles were missing.

He searched for a few minutes longer and presently found the other one on the floor of the tiny kitchen, back in a corner under the sink. A speck of dried blood on its point.

Or was it blood?

Police, he thought. I should go and notify the police. But the next moment he knew he couldn't. He couldn't afford any questioning. He could not risk being detained. He must not get in a position which might force him to reveal his true identity. It was certain he would be held for questioning, if not for murder. He wondered if anyone had known that he was to come here. It might well be a trap to put him on the spot!

Even if it was true that she had committed suicide . . . he must not be questioned. His papers were in order .

. . Paul Mercier from Marseilles. Department— Thirty-nine years old. Anybody would believe those extra ten years. Salesman. Released from a German prison camp May 10. His accent was perfect. He had spoken the language with his French mother since early childhood. His father had objected a little at first but later had realized the value. Three years or almost three years in France before the war had taken the last trace of accent away. Yet . . . Chet still did not want any questions.

He looked once more at the Vachon, then setting his teeth and quite unconsciously making a small gesture of salute, he went out of the kitchen, through the one room, and cautiously opened the door. The floor was empty. He hurried down to the first landing, heard steps and withdrew quickly into the lavatory at the end of the corridor. After a few minutes when everything seemed quiet again, he went out and on.

The courtyard was empty. The musicians had left and the onlookers had withdrawn from the windows. He crossed the cobblestones quickly. The cage of the caretaker was still empty. He pushed through the old-fashioned large front door and out to the street. Only then he noticed that he was still clutching the little bunch of lilies of the valley he had bought a good half hour ago at the corner, as he watched the pigeons sailing across the church of Sacré-Coeur.

He didn't dare to go back to his rented room. All evening long he sat in little cafés and bistros, changing them quickly, waiting for the evening papers. What would they say about the death of the Vachon? Murder or suicide? There was nothing in the papers.

When night fell he went on and over to the left side of the Seine. Once before he had slept under a bridge. But tonight, as years ago, policemen walking in pairs were patrolling the streets. He could not afford to take the chance.

So he walked, kept on walking with the air of a man who knew where he was going. He decided if anyone stopped him he would say the Atala. The Atala. Sue, he thought. Then I would see you and you would say yes, we were on our honeymoon.

He almost wished at a certain period, in the early hours of dawn, that someone would stop him and ask him. But no one did.

He saw the carts come into the city, pitifully few compared with the cavalcade which before the war had rumbled into Paris from late evening on in the direction of the Halles to offer the fruits of the land; vegetables, fruits, meat.

Now all he counted were two milk trucks and three old covered wagons.

Finally he saw the gnomelike figures of undernourished children, bent double under the heavy burden of the morning newspapers, trotting along to their destinations.

Chet bought several and, sitting on a staircase of a public building in the first beams of sunlight, he lit a cigarette.

He turned the pages carefully. No mention of Josephine and her death. No human interest story of the suicide of a famous old Cancan dancer of the music hall.

During the day Chet slept in the subway, being

carried forward through Paris from east to west and north to south. There still was nothing about Josephine in the noon papers. Then in the evening, exactly twenty-four hours after he had discovered her hanging from the hook in her tiny kitchen, he found a small notice listed under Obituaries.

Vachon, Josephine. 56 years old. Today at her residence.

Vachon, Josephine . . . no mention of occupation, no mention of cause of death, nothing.

Whoever was guilty of her death possessed sufficient power and influence to keep the details out of the news.

In the pockets of his jacket Chet's hands formed fists. He knew that she had been murdered . . . and by someone powerful enough to suppress the fact of murder. There would be no charge or pursuit.

2

Maybe it was the lilies of the valley he had bought for Josephine which gave him the idea when he found them unexpectedly, now dried and brown, in one of his trouser pockets.

There had been lilies of the valley near the little village where he had landed that early dawn. He could remember quite clearly seeing those small white bells nestling in the shelter of their long dark-green leaves in the little wood through which he had been marched.

It had been spring then as it was now. The stone wall . . . the lilac, pink and purple and white.

There was also the realization that, without Josephine, he did not know how and with whom he should get in contact. Her vague promise of possible help had died with her. Suddenly it seemed logical and probable that, at the very place where he had been betrayed, he might find people who might remember what had happened there, almost four years ago . . . people who might remember names and incidents, and who might be willing to talk.

Nobody could possibly suspect a newly released prisoner of war checking to see if his old uncle Mercier was still alive. Were there not thousands of people wandering over the world trying to find out what had happened to their relatives, loved ones, anyone who belonged to them?

Trains were still running sparsely, tracks were still being repaired. After a day of fruitless attempts to secure a ticket, Chet gave up his idea of traveling by railroad.

His colonel had furnished him with money. By paying three times its value he managed to talk his landlady into selling him her daughter's bicycle.

From Paris to N— was only eighty miles. He remembered exactly, vividly, the map he had studied years before in London. Every little blue and pink and green spot; the river, the stretches of wood, the winding of the highway and the little paths which ran along it. It was the last thing he had looked upon while at liberty.

He pedaled along the Loire through the spring. People were tilling the soil, rebuilding destroyed houses, cleaning away the rubbish of mortar and brick and twisted iron. People were sitting alongside the road, tired and homeless, or just dozing in the sweet warm sunshine or waiting for an opportunity to hitch a ride to the next village or town.

The first night he spent in a peasant's hut, the second in the open under a clear starry sky with a fat white moon over an almost noiseless landscape. Only the frogs and the crickets and the soft murmur of the river and the smell of young leaves and spring flowers and the soil and the memory of Susan feeding the monkeys in the Central Park Zoo.

Towards evening of the third day he saw the contours of four round heavy towers against the pale dusk of the sky. He stopped pedaling and sprang from his seat. There it was. The landmark! The famous castle of N—. He remembered another time, another day when, as a student, he had stopped in front of the wide moat which surrounded it. Though it was open to the public on two days it was still privately owned, and he had joined a group of sightseers who waited for the drawbridge to lower. The guide had asked them to be patient; the old duchess had ruled that she was not to be disturbed by the thunder of the old wooden construction as long as she was asleep. The guide had said it proudly, almost as if this order increased the value of the castle. An old, sad elephant had wandered across a meadow beyond the water. And again the guide had been proud to point out the animal as a present of one illustrious guest.

Not quite three miles to the east of the castle lay the village; then, as now, his original destination.

It was a small village with a little pond at one end.

A few ducks were slipping into the dirty water as Chet passed it. A large pink pig trotted slowly away and, in the back yard of a house, a dog on a long chain barked furiously.

The main street looked surprisingly townlike. There were several two-story buildings, some shops, the post office and, formerly, two hotels. The last two had been destroyed completely. Children were playing in the rubble. The post office still stood but had lost its roof, its windows, and one of its walls had caved in.

At the other end of the village he knew must be the inn he had liked so much on his first visit, if it was still there.

A few minutes later he saw it. Only the big tree with a bench around its wide trunk had been hit, and the burned crown seemed to point accusingly at a civilization which had killed it in its pride and beauty long before its destined end.

He locked his bicycle wheel and leaned it against the house wall.

At the left of the entrance lay the dining room, on the right, the bar. A long counter of plain brown wood ran along its whole length. There were several small tables and chairs along one side. It was completely empty.

Chet knocked against the wood of one table and after a while, when nobody appeared, called, "Anybody in?"

From the back of the room a voice answered sullenly, "What's the hurry?"

A door opened and, with the smell of the kitchen, a heavily built man came in. Like Josephine, he wore slippers and just as hers had, they made a soft slurring sound on the bare floor. In the half-dark of the room Chet imagined he could see the Vachon, in her shiny black raincoat, hanging from a hook in her kitchen.

"I've got nothing," the man said. "No cigarettes, no wine, no food for strangers. The restaurant is closed."

Chet turned. "I just wanted a glass of beer and possibly a room for tonight."

"Got money?" asked his host, giving him a quick shrewd look. Chet took a bill from his wallet and waved it gently across the counter. Then, putting it back, he brought out some cigarettes and watched the man's glance shift from his face to his hands. He held out the cigarettes. The man took one and broke it into careful halves, one of which he stuck behind is left ear, the other one he lit. Then, extending the flame of the match to Chet, he called over his shoulder, "Marie, see if there is a bottle of beer left in the well." Slowly he brought two glasses out from under the counter and, sliding one along towards Chet, said casually:

"So you want a room?"

"Just for tonight. Or maybe two."

"It's a long time since we had guests. Once it paid to stay open summer and winter to run this place . . ." He broke off and Chet could see the desperation in his eyes.

A woman came in. Chet could hardly recognize the once proud proprietress: Madame, in her black silk dress and a pince-nez, sitting on a high chair behind the little cashier's cage, ruling, with a move of her eyelashes, the waiters and girls who served. But the dignity which she had possessed then had not left her, though everything else about her had grown poor and shabby and old and tired. She put a bottle of beer down on the counter, looking at Chester curiously.

"From Paris?" she said. "You are from Paris, aren't you? I saw the number of your bicycle and the stamp. Tell me, tell me . . . there are still prisoners coming in?"

"Of course they're coming in, Marie," interrupted the man in a way that showed how often during days and nights he had replied to the same question with the same answer. "Didn't you hear the radio? They said . . ." But now he, too, looked at Chet, forgetting to pour the beer which he had opened.

"I just came back myself," said Chester. "Only last week. There is so much red tape connected with it, so much checking up and . . ."

"You came back? Back from where . . . ?"

"Germany," he said. "I was a prisoner of war for three years."

The woman's hand on the counter began to tremble violently. She tried to speak and then looked at her husband appealingly. He said slowly:

"We have a son, our only son. They took him. We haven't heard from him for over a year."

"That doesn't mean that he is not alive," Chet said quickly. "In my camp they wouldn't even allow the Red Cross messages."

"And where were you? Our son's name is Theophile. Theophile Lebrun. Did you ever hear of a Theophile Lebrun?"

Chet shook his head, but though he couldn't give them any news, half an hour later he sat down with them in the large old-fashioned kitchen for the evening meal. Slowly, carefully, he was feeling his way.

"There is no one of my family in Marseilles alive. All killed in bombings, they told me. All of my people. The house gone, the shop gone, nothing but rubble." He shrugged his shoulders. "So then I remembered an old uncle. He moved away long before the war. To somewhere around here. I was here once before—but I've forgotten where he worked. He was a gardener. His name was Mercier. Paul Mercier. I am called after him."

"Mercier?" repeated Lebrun and got up to fill their glasses with some red wine which had appeared miraculously from under a trap door in the kitchen floor.

"Mercier. Of course I remember him. He was here only a few years before the whole mess started. Over there," he pointed vaguely, "taking care of Monsieur Blois's garden."

The name slashed like a knife into Chet's consciousness.

"Blois," he repeated. "Blois. Of course, that was the name. Pierre . . . Pierre Blois."

"That's correct," confirmed Madame Lebrun. "Pierre Blois. I remember when he first came here. He dined here that night. Just a little while before your uncle came. 1936, wasn't it? The summer of 1936. He was here with the lawyer, old man Braque, who later shot himself to escape the Germans. It was then that he bought the little estate a few miles further down than the castle. He got the water rights too, I remember."

Again in his mind Chet saw the map, the diagram

of the landing place. "A few miles further down than the castle. A branch of the river runs along one side of the meadow. You'll find it a safe place. It belongs to one of the most trusted . . ."

"He's a big shot now," Lebrun was saying. "Well, I guess he deserves it. Active man. Good man. Did a lot for the people around here, always progressive, he . . . they say if it were not for him a lot more people would be dead. He served France well."

"So did your uncle," his wife broke in, and she smiled at Chet. "He was a fine upright man, knew his profession as nobody else. He had a hand with things. Green fingers. Plants that seemed doomed came back under his care. And he gave his life for France. He belonged to the maquis. Hush . . . it's all right," she reminded her husband, and again she smiled. "It's hard sometimes to remember that now we can speak openly. No longer do we need to be afraid of traitors."

Chet suppressed the flood of questions he wanted to hurl at them. He knew he must go slowly. He put his arms on the table and buried his head in them. The Lebruns realized suddenly that, without any preparation, they had told him that his uncle, whom he had hoped to find alive, was dead. An awkward silence fell. Then finally, Chet lifted his head and, gazing into space, said:

"I am glad he worked with the maquis. I only hope that he wasn't betrayed?"

The silence lingered on and he saw by the changing expression of their faces that, though they had been eager to break it with sympathy, his last sentence had stopped them.

He looked from one to the other but, unlike Josephine, they did not seem to be afraid, only uneasy.

"Who can tell now?" Madame Lebrun said. "There was some talk but who can tell?"

"Talk? About what?" asked Chet and suddenly he did not dare to light a cigarette for fear his shaking hands might betray his eagerness. Then he remembered that shaky hands were a legitimate property of a prisoner of war.

"About the night he died."

"Shot by the Germans, of course."

Both of them were talking now, interrupting each other, helping each other to remember.

"One night when they caught an American. We didn't know about it then, but later it leaked out."

"You see, Mercier, we were pretty lucky around here. There was a detention camp for French prisoners before they were sent away, but no Gestapo."

"And then they came, suddenly. I can still hear their sirens screaming and then their cars shot past the inn. They killed little Francoise who was playing in the street and couldn't get away in time."

"And where do you think they went? To Pierre Blois's house. They took it over completely. They were quartered there."

"And then?" asked Chet, his voice level, politely curious. He took another sip of his wine, old, dead wine.

"After a short while they left. This district was not very important, you see, and by that time the prisoners had been shifted. The best of our men shipped into Germany. There only remained the military, and they were billeted at the castle. Swine!"

"And the American?"

"They said he was a spy and we heard that he wouldn't speak. So then they shot him."

"Just before an air raid," Lebrun threw in.

"We only had a few. You see there was nothing here which was of importance."

"That was the night your uncle died."

"But some said—Christine said—they shot your uncle before they caught the American."

Now Chet lit a cigarette, forgetting to offer Lebrun one.

"Who is Christine?"

He saw Lebrun's eyes follow the curl of smoke from his cigarette, remembered and pushed the package over to him.

"She was a maid in the house, and the Germans kept her on when they took it over. She said she saw two men going into Mercier's little cottage—he lived right next to the entrance—two hours before it all happened."

"Well, she is dead now. They—well, she was a pretty girl . . . a very pretty girl and so young."

"It doesn't need to be true . . ."

Madame Lebrun pushed her chair aside and got up, went over to the big old-fashioned hearth where only one single opening was alive with a small flame and lifted a blue chipped enamel coffeepot.

"The whole thing must have been a trap," she said. Her voice echoed against the white chalked walls and back from the beamed ceiling.

"I remember exactly. They announced a curfew the

day before. Everyone who was seen outside after five o'clock in the afternoon would be shot on sight. It was spring and we were busy with the seedlings. After three days they lifted it. But why should there have been a curfew between five in the evening and five in the morning when before . . ."

She misunderstood Chet's intent frown of concentration and explained, "We are talking about the night they caught the American."

"They say they took him the moment he came down in his parachute," Lebrun interrupted. "They let him land all right, no antiaircraft, no lights . . . sure, he was betrayed."

"But by whom?" asked Madame Lebrun.

Her husband shrugged his shoulders. "We'll never know."

Chet swallowed the first sip of the hot, bitter chicory-tasting coffee. He knew that, peasant-like, they had worried this subject for years.

"I always suspected the Mole," Madame said.

Chet set down his cup. "Who is the Mole?" he asked.

"It's wrong of you, Marie, to say something like that about a man, just because . . ." Lebrun looked at his wife reproachfully, shaking his head. "Just because you don't like him is no reason to . . ."

"I don't trust him," retorted Madame Lebrun and her eyes narrowed to pinpoints, reminding Chet of Josephine Vachon's eyes when she had looked at him and through him.

"He's the caretaker of the estate," Madame Lebrun went on as if defying her husband. "He got the job late in the fall of '39. Just two months after Germany went to war. I don't trust him," she said again.

"It's not very wise to speak against a man who has Monsieur Blois's confidence. He's the only one around here who's got money. We have to stay on good terms with him. If he should hear that you had said . . ."

"You think he knew my uncle?" Chester asked.

"Why, of course he did. They worked together. Sure he knew him."

"Maybe he could tell me about him, about his last days . . ."

"Maybe. He's not easy to converse with. He isn't the talking kind."

"No," agreed Lebrun, "but maybe in a case like this . . ."

Chet was given the same little room he had slept in on his first stay at the inn. Only this time he did not sleep. The room was the same, a small quadrangle with a wide bed and two chairs and one small table. But now there were no white organdy curtains at the windows, no linen on the mattress, and the wallpaper had faded. The quaint old pattern of stagecoaches, lovely miller girls and young gentlemen was only vaguely recognizable.

He lay in the dark, smoking, thinking, sometime, in the dead silence of the house hearing voices out of the past.

"You'll find it a safe place . . . it belongs to one of our most trusted members . . ." And it had been and was Pierre Blois's house. Chet tried to recall Pierre Blois's face as he had seen it in London and then again when he had seen it in Paris as he sat on the bench next to the old veteran. A large, wide, forceful face. A high forehead, small narrow eyes above an arrogant, crooked nose, a long chin which always seemed to be set in a purpose. And Josephine Vachon's sullen, resigned words: "The wrong people always get in. We . . ."

"I am crazy," Chester told himself, remembering what his colonel had said, the veteran had said, even Lebrun had said this evening . . . that the man was hero, had served France, had distinguished himself.

No. No. No. But then there had been only two men who had known details besides himself and his colonel. Pierre Blois and the other in France . . . the link in the chain. But hadn't Josephine refused the name of the man who had given her orders? "I don't remember." She had known something about that other man, something which was dangerous to know. Pierre Blois simply had given his house and estate to be used in the mission, trusting the people he had left in charge of it.

Tomorrow, decided Chester, tomorrow I will speak to the Mole.

There was the stone wall, dividing the property, running clear through a wide green meadow, more than ever reminding Chet of a stone fence in New York State. And there the lilac bush now, as it had been then—in full bloom, pink and purple and fragrant, with tiny moths fluttering around it.

"If you try the entrance, he won't even let you in," Madame Lebrun had said, when that morning she had surprisingly entered his room, carrying a tray with a cup of hot milk, faintly tinted with brown, and a piece of bread. She had smiled then a little bashfully.

"I keep on thinking Theophile is back and how he would want to stretch out in bed and have his breakfast brought up and feel safe and coddled."

And she began to cry softly. "Tell me, but tell me the truth, is it true what the papers say . . . about all those atrocities . . . they—they—they're showing pictures. I couldn't go."

Chet had not answered right away. He had lain in the soft sheetless bed and thought of his own confinement. He wanted to say, "It's true! It's more than true. It's worse than the films they show. Believe it all, believe it forever, don't forget it. It's true." But Marie Lebrun was a mother with a son from whom she had not heard for more than a year, and so he had remained silent till finally he had pointed at himself. "Look at me. I came back. It was bad. But I came back. Only a few days ago." He told her then that he wanted to go down to talk to the Mole.

"Go through the meadows," Madame Lebrun had advised him. "Just swing over the wall. It's low and no trouble, and you will be in the garden and near the cottage where your uncle lived."

He stood still. For a few moments the stone wall was no longer part of a French landscape somewhere around the river Loire, but a stone wall near the Hudson and Sue was sitting on it. Sue, wearing white and blue striped shorts and a white blouse open at the throat. Her short curly hair was a shade deeper because it was still wet from swimming in the river, and she was singing a silly little song because it was a beautiful day and they were together and young and happy with no worries in the world.

"There came a lizard to the wall . . ."

He could hear her now. Her voice light and lovely, rising. But what he heard was a bird singing through the blue of a morning in May, singing high above his head. The vision faded, the memory went; tension remained.

He saw the Mole as soon as he vaulted the fence.

The man was standing near the gardener's lodging, splitting wood. He was a broad, sturdily built man with bulging muscles. They stood out on his bare forearms as he swung the ax expertly. He had a face Chet did not like . . . a cruel face, with the hair growing deep into a low square forehead over narrow eyes. Everything was narrow about his face, his nostrils, even his mouth a thin narrow line. Only the hair and the eyebrows and the black hair on his bare arms and hands were abundant.

"He comes from the Vendée," Madame Lebrun had said, sitting primly erect on one of the two chairs in his room, watching him drinking the milk and dipping the bread into the cup. "He comes from the Vendée." As if that were enough, a whole long explanation. The Vendée—a part of middle France which was known to breed stingy, sullen people—stingy, sullen and passionate. Some of the worst murderers in the criminal history of France had been born in the Vendée.

"*Bonjour*," Chet said now. "A nice morning, isn't it?" The man did not look up but continued to split the wood. Chet tried the trick with his cigarettes again, lighting one obviously, blowing a cloud of smoke in the direction of the man. There was no reaction.

"Nice place!" Chet glanced towards the little lodge into which, four years ago, he had crawled, weak and bleeding. "Big estate, is it?"

The Mole stuck the ax into the log, yawned, stretched and growled:

"I am the caretaker here and this is private property and we don't like people snooping around."

He began throwing piece after piece of wood on the neatly stacked pile.

"But such a big place," said Chet. "Isn't it hard to take care of alone?"

"If you're after a job," answered the Mole, "I have nothing for you. I can manage by myself." He worked on as if Chet did not exist.

Chet walked around the man and the woodpile and leaned against a tree opposite the Mole. "My uncle used to work here," he said.

There was no answer.

"Always wanted to see the place," he persisted. "Though I was held here in the nearby camp before I was shipped into Germany. Just came back."

Silence. The woodpile grew higher.

Chet tried again.

"It's so peaceful here. A place I would like."

"I have no job for you," repeated the Mole. His voice was as sullen and unprepossessing as his face. Chet had not known exactly what to say to the Mole, had decided to wait to see how the conversation would run. Now he changed his tactics.

"I didn't come to ask for a job," he said hesitantly, watching the Mole closely. But the heavy face remained empty, sullen.

"I didn't come here for a job," Chet repeated.

"Then go away."

"I wanted to talk to you."

"I don't know you," said the Mole. "Never seen you around here before and I don't talk to strangers."

He sat down on the stump and wiped his face with a filthy cloth. "There are dogs here," he added without changing his voice. "They don't like strangers either."

Chester looked across the stone fence out into the meadow where buttercups looked like golden flyspecks on a green carpet. Dogs? Did the man think he could frighten him away? Dogs? He remembered the dogs German guards had set upon people too weak to march, too weak to work or so afraid of dying that they had clung to the ground where they had fallen.

Chet said abruptly:

"Do you remember the night the Gestapo caught an American here? Right here?"

The Mole got up and resumed his work.

"The Gestapo caught many Americans," he said.

"In the beginning? I heard in the village that the Gestapo was here only once. Weren't you here then? Weren't you?"

He paused because suddenly he knew that he had seen the man before. Just for a second, but he had seen the big red mole on his left cheek. How could he have forgotten? The man had been in the hall of the house, the house which lay about three hundred yards back of where he was sitting, and the red roof and chimney of which he could see clearly between the branches of trees. The Mole had been there in the hall when four men had taken him up the staircase into a wide, gracious room for his first questioning. They had been frighteningly polite then, making a cat-and-mouse farce of his capture. But in the mass of brutal faces, in his own confusion and tension, his brain working rapidly, his body chilling with imagination of what would probably happen to him and to all those connected with him, he had not seen as clearly then as he did now in retrospect.

"What makes you think so?" asked the Mole as his ax split the air viciously.

"I told you. I was over at the prison camp. I saw you pass it day after day."

"So what? Why all the questions? The American is dead."

The bird was still singing, high and sweet.

"I knew him," said Chet. "They put him into our barracks for a couple of nights. They wanted to see if he would speak, if he would talk to us. But he was careful. They took him out after that and I never saw him again."

"He is dead," repeated the Mole and now for the first time he glanced up and fixed his narrow eyes on Chet.

"What makes you so interested in a dead American?"

Chester stared at a small ant heap through which the tiny insects were moving, imperturbably carrying on with their work.

"He was betrayed, wasn't he?"

"Was he?" asked the Mole. "I wouldn't know."

"We were speculating at the camp about it. Remember the sudden curfew, the sudden appearance the Gestapo put in. They must have been waiting for him. They must have known he was coming. And I heard some of his guards talking in front of our barracks. Things like that stick in one's mind."

The Mole again stopped working; he put his hand into his pocket and brought forth some loose tobacco and a small slip of paper. He rolled the cigarette with one hand, quickly, not losing one crumb of tobacco. He licked the glued edge of paper and pushed the cigarette with his tongue between his lips and lighted it.

"If I were you," he said slowly, "I would let the dead rest where they are. Why bother about the dead?"

Chester's eyes were on the meadow. Somewhere under the fresh young green grass close to the wall ten other men had been shot. Where had they been buried?

"Men expect to die in war," he answered. "But they expect to be killed by the enemy, not by those they came to help."

"The Germans killed him. I told you that. They shot him."

"That is only secondary, the way I see it." Chester moved his foot into another position, careful not to crush the ants and the castle they were building for their queen. "He was killed by the people who betrayed him. They caused his death. The Germans only fired the guns."

"I don't know what you mean. Let the dead be dead and buried, I tell you. He's dead. Why bother, why bother if he was betrayed and who betrayed him?"

There was the same evasiveness in his sullen voice and face. Chet couldn't figure the man out.

"Why bother?" he repeated. "Why? What did we fight for? What did I spend three years in Germany for?

What did our wives and children and parents die for? What were we hungry for? And cold? What was our country ruined for? Why did men and women all over the world die?"

"I don't know what you mean."

"Of course we have to bother. Aren't we going to make a clean sweep of everything? Didn't we fight the fascists, and those who played along with the Germans, the opportunists, the cowards? If we were betrayed, any of us, we should band together and find those who betrayed us and our cause."

The Mole said nothing. Then, unexpectedly after a pause, he shrugged his shoulders. "Who knows?" he said. "Who can know? There were lots of different characters in the maquis."

"You worked with them?"

The Mole spat out a big, solid piece of phlegm. "What do you think?" he snapped. "Of course I did. We all did. Every decent Frenchman did. Go home, I tell you, wherever you come from. I couldn't tell you anything. I don't know anything." He looked up slyly, sizing Chet up. "Grandelieu should know," he said. "Why don't you ask Grandelieu? Maybe he knows. He knew a lot."

"Who is Grandelieu?"

The Mole laughed. It sounded like a snort. "He used to give orders around here, around this district. One of the top men. Dr. Grandelieu from Paris."

There was a truck with lumber under its wide green tarpaulin going in the direction of Paris. The driver had stopped for a drink at the old inn and Monsieur Lebrun had talked him into giving Paul Mercier a ride.

Chet was glad to leave. Somehow the last day he had spent in the village had been unpleasant. At first people had been interested in him, asking a thousand questions about his experience in Germany, recalling incidents which had happened to them during the occupation. Then, at some indefinite moment, they had lost interest. And their fear that he, because he was the first in their neighborhood to come back, would get a job, the opportunity to work and make money, had suddenly become obvious.

They had their own worries, their own affairs to attend to. He'd questioned two more men from the neighborhood. One of them knew nothing, the other confirmed what the Mole had said, that a doctor from Paris, a man called Grandelieu, had given orders in that district.

In vain Chet had tried to find a trace of the old woman who had nursed him and hidden him. She seemed to have disappeared from the earth as well as from the memory of the villagers. And yet she had not been a hallucination of feverish dreams. He could remember her face very clearly, old and wrinkled with a mustache on her upper lip, a few yellow teeth, and eternally moving jaws as she chewed an invisible cud.

But the chief unpleasantness had come from something entirely apart from his failures.

Chet turned his head and looked back out of the window, across his bicycle which lay on top, tied to the tarpaulin. The rare sight of a motorcycle appeared far down the highway. It came rapidly closer and he recognized the uniform of a policeman, but as it passed the slow-moving truck he also saw that another person was sitting in the small sidecar.

It was the same man he had spotted at the inn after his return from the Mole, and had again seen when he took a walk later in the afternoon.

A small man whose body seemed to consist of rubber instead of bones, who moved with incredibly silent speed and somehow reminded Chet of the large black cat in Josephine's drafty dressing room. His face, childishly young, was expressionless. Only a few hours before Chet had seen him still once more, sitting on the bench under the scarred tree, studying the many large and small carvings people had cut into the bark. To his question Madame Lebrun had answered: "Jacques? Oh, he's been around for some time. Used to work in a circus as a trapeze artist and then he fell. They say he's not quite right in his head. The fall, you know."

Now Jacques was sitting next to the policeman, riding, like Chet, towards Paris, or at least in the direction of Paris.

Was he being watched? Was he being followed? Nonsense, thought Chester. Why should anyone follow me?

The driver beside him was obviously nervous. Every time Chet moved or pushed his hands into his pockets the man's jaw set. Following his flickering glance Chet saw that the man wasn't watching the road in the mirror but had moved the small reflector in such a way that no movement Chet made could escape his eyes.

He tried to talk to the man, who seemed determined

not to be distracted from his vigilance. And only when he was dropped in the outskirts of Paris did the man's expression change; and when Chet offered him some money and a few cigarettes, he stared in bewilderment. Suddenly a loud, roaring laugh eased his chest.

"*Zut*," he said. "And I was afraid you might bang me over the head and steal my money and the truck. No offense meant. You never know what kind of people bum a ride nowadays. When people are poor and hungry . . . well, if Monsieur Lebrun hadn't asked me to take you along I would never have done so."

The scars of war. The distrust, the wolfishness, the fear.

Almost opposite from where Chet was dropped he saw the sober outlines of a post office building. He had to wait quite a while in line before it was his turn at one of the many city directories which listed the inhabitants of Paris. Soldiers, French as well as American and British, Red Cross workers and civilians were looking up addresses, their faces intent, eager.

Grandelieu, B. R. Grandelieu . . .

Chester copied the address carefully into his small notebook. Blois or Grandelieu? Blois or Grandelieu? His mind kept on spinning. One of the two. Blois knew, that much he was sure of. Grandelieu gave the orders in the neighborhood in which he had been caught.

But was Grandelieu, B. R. Grandelieu, identical with the man whose code name had been "Half Moon?"

It was not a fashionable address. On the contrary. Dr. Grandelieu's office was situated in a workers' district in the east of the city, a neighborhood which

Chet hardly knew. Here factories and big wholesale markets dominated the scene. Tenement houses, some of them utterly destroyed, some under repair, lined the big ugly street. There was no beauty anywhere, no lovely old church or even a building to demonstrate the artisanship of earlier centuries. No proudly arched bridge, no carved woodwork. Even the sky seemed less high, less wide, less blue. Street vendors shouting the prices of their shabby wares, beggars, women sitting on little stools sharpening knives for a few cents, half-starved dogs, dirty children and the empty stalls in front of shops. Reeling drunken men, thin and heavily painted girls with stockingless legs and high heels.

In the entrance of one of the dreary buildings was the sign: DOCTEUR GRANDELIEU. *Ground Floor*.

Chet was surprised to find that the waiting room was large, clean and comfortable. The walls were freshly painted, a soft cool blue. Wide benches covered with oilcloth ran along their full length. A shelf holding magazines, books and games. Several small tables and lamps and even some fresh flowers on the window sill, small yellow tulips just opening.

Almost every place was taken. There were about thirty people lining the walls. All of them shabbily dressed, wearing, in addition to their pains and worries, the signs of poverty. A man moved when Chet entered and he sat down. A few minutes later an elderly nurse came into the waiting room, smiled pleasantly and asked:

"Who is next, please?"

Chet half rose, and she said quickly:

"The doctor will see you in turn. But, of course, if you need immediate attention . . . ? This is your first time here, isn't it?"

Chet nodded. "Thank you, I can wait."

The woman next to him smiled, turning to look at him with open curiosity. "New, eh? Well, sometimes I wish they would not spread his name all over and send others here. But then, of course, he's the good angel of the poor."

The good angel of the poor? thought Chet. Grandelieu, the good angel of the poor. He realized that subconsciously he had expected a different establishment. A swanky place with a few rich patients and crisp, efficient nurses, in a neighborhood which was luxurious and expensive. But most certainly not this.

The good angel of the poor?

Prices in Paris were exorbitant, and medical supplies almost unobtainable. How could Dr. Grandelieu afford to be the angel of the poor, to treat them apparently for nothing?

Slowly the hours moved. Broken snatches of conversation hit his ear. Two or three times he chatted with one of the other patients, biding his time, listening patiently to their stories of their ailments before asking them cautious questions about the doctor. None of them who was not full of praise for the man. All through the war he had kept on working, in raids and shellfire. Defying curfew, Germans and bombings alike wherever he was needed.

Nearly two hours had passed before the nurse beckoned to him. "I believe it's your turn. The doctor will see you now."

The inner office was furnished with surprisingly modern equipment. For a second, Chet's thoughts wandered back and into the small room in which Sue's father had treated his patients. The Porters had never been wealthy, and when they first moved to Elmira the living room had been turned into the office. Dr. Porter had dreamed of an office like this.

The nurse sat down behind a small writing desk asking for his name, explaining that they preferred to take personal histories in private.

"The doctor will be right back," she said when she had completed his card. "I persuaded him to eat something. It's almost four o'clock and he had neither breakfast nor luncheon."

When she left the room Chet walked around curiously. Except for a few framed diplomas which showed that Grandelieu had been graduated from the Sorbonne, studied a term in Germany, at Munich, there was nothing personal. But as he turned round he suddenly found himself facing the writing desk from another direction. His card lay on it, held down by a curiously shaped silver paperweight. It was a half disc. He moved closer and saw the inscription. He felt his heart hammering in his throat as he bent over.

"To Half Moon, in memory. P. B."

The room and its medical equipment faded into a blacked-out London office. "You can trust Half Moon!" P. B.—Pierre Blois.

"To Half Moon, in memory."

To Half Moon!

So Half Moon, the man he had been told to contact, and Dr. Grandelieu were one and the same person. One and the same man.

Chester Burton sat down on the nearest chair. He stared absent-mindedly at a fluoroscope in the corner opposite him.

The quiet clean office suddenly was filled with voices. His own, asking questions, others answering. "Who was the man who gave you orders, Josephine?"

"I don't remember. I told you my memory was bad."

"Why don't you ask Grandelieu? He should know. He used to give orders around here."

"You see, we were lucky. The Gestapo came here only for a short time. Just a few days before the night they caught the American."

"Some say he didn't die in the raid, he was shot before . . ." And his colonel's voice, "I don't think we ever knew the identity of Blois's man in France beyond his code name but I have not forgotten that there was never any reason to doubt him."

From nearby he heard the opening and the closing of a door. A warm deep voice greeting a patient in the waiting room. Chet rose, tense, facing the door. Light steps coming closer and closer. He saw the handle of the door move, slowly, the door opening, the high long back of a man, broad in the shoulders, smaller around the hips. The back of his head, turned still towards the waiting room, thick black hair, the clean-shaved neck above the collarless white jacket.

The man turned now, pulled the door shut and offered his hand.

"The nurse told me that you're just back in France

after a three-year hell in Germany. I am happy you came to me. What can I do for you?"

He had an unexpectedly young and handsome face. A high wide forehead, large beautifully shaped eyes with lashes almost girlishly long and full, a short straight nose and a nice mouth set above a firm round chin. He was pale and looked strained but his eyes were smiling, smiling straight into Chet's.

Chet stood motionless, unable for a minute to move, to find words, to say anything. All he was conscious of was the last time he had seen this face. The same face. Not long ago. Oh no, not long ago. A week ago, the evening he had gone to see Josephine at the music hall.

It was the face of the man who had sat next to Sue, the same man to whom she had said in that unmistakable way:

"Of course I do, Robert."

3

Just around the corner of a side street, a block away from the Champs-Elysées and near to the Étoile and the Arc de Triomphe, was the little hotel in which Sue lived.

Chet had followed her for more than two hours until she disappeared into the Atala. Two hours before he had been thinking so intently of her that when he had suddenly seen her in front of him at a newspaper stall buying a magazine, he had, for a moment, imagined her a vision in his thoughts and not a reality.

She wore no hat. Chet remembered her saying that she had never owned one except for an Easter bonnet on her tenth birthday. The bag she carried was strapped on two narrow ribbons to her shoulders and swayed gently with every step she took. She was dressed in something blue and soft with little white frills around the throat and wrists, and her feet, those small feet of which she was so proud, thrust in some sort of blue sandals. Blue and golden she seemed to be, a bit of sunny sky fallen to the earth, but Chet following closely behind her saw another Sue in front of him. A little Sue in a bulky snow suit, red-cheeked and yelling, her blond curls dancing, building a snow man in the back yard of the boy next door.

But they were both the same Sue: the child grown into a young woman who had lost the boy she had intended to marry; who had to amputate a past world which held no future from her heart and mind, burying dreams and hopes; who finally, alone and, perhaps, lost in a present of hard realities, had fallen in love with Robert Grandelieu.

Pierre Blois or Robert Grandelieu? Pierre Blois or Robert Grandelieu? Pierre Blois or Robert Grandelieu? One of the two. One or the other. And everything pointed to Grandelieu. To Grandelieu, the man she loved, to whom she had said, "Of course I do."

And if he, Chet, discovered the proof that it was Grandelieu as he assumed; then this man, the second man in her life, would be exposed to the whole world, would go on trial for treason, Intelligence with the enemy, collaboration with the Germans, would be condemned and probably executed.

The man who had taken his place in her heart and mind, and her dreams and plans for the future, would die, too . . . a traitor, a spy, a despicable death.

She must be warned. Somehow she must be prepared. Before it was too late, before she was engaged to him or perhaps married, before the world knew of their relationship; before the world could drag in Susan Porter.

That, at least, she must be spared.

But if she was warned anonymously or by a stranger, would she not tell Grandelieu? Would she not immediately warn him in her loyal indignation? And wouldn't Grandelieu, unsuspected except by Chet, easily find a way to rob Chet of the chance to expose him, to prove his guilt?

Once, in a crowd of people milling around a subway station, Chet thought he saw again the rubberlike boneless movements of the man with the face of a child, but he was too deeply concerned with Sue and himself to pay much attention.

Forget your own aims for a moment, Chet, and think of Sue. Only of Sue and how such a mess might affect her. How did he know how deeply she had suffered in the past year after his death was announced officially, or in the years of doubt before? How did he know if and to what extent she could absorb another bad shock?

How could he?

But she must be warned about Grandelieu. And then? With what was she left then . . . if not . . . if not . . . if not.

If there was no substitute, someone to whom she could turn?

But if Sue were to know that he, that Chet, the boy she had loved, was alive, not dead, not buried in an unknown grave, but there in front of her, returned from death to love her with all his heart?

Then there was not so much of a problem any longer. Then the loss of Robert Grandelieu might not harm her quite so much. Then . . . then he, Chet, could pursue his task without too much danger of her suffering or having Grandelieu warned by an unsuspecting Sue.

She could help him, sharing his secret; she would help him and keep quiet. Keep quiet until the time came when he was officially alive again. And, if something should happen to him, if he should be killed after all, as Josephine had been murdered, they, Sue and he, would have known some happiness and most certainly she would have been spared some of the disillusionment over Grandelieu.

It seemed so simple, so logical, the only thing to do. He ignored any deterrents against such action on his part. He was not superhuman, he might be a man with a tough job to do, but he was also a man deeply in love.

As Chet watched Sue disappear through the entrance of the hotel, he had reached the decision to see her. All that now remained was a wide and happy dream of how it would be to see her again, to take her into his arms, to feel her lips.

The anticipation of the moment was too strong. He walked around the entire block twice before he felt calm enough to enter the small lobby of the hotel and cross to the desk.

The old clerk behind it was still the same one who, many years ago, had told a young student how to get most quickly to the Café of the Deux Magots. A little older, a little grayer, more than ever looking like a molting owl, his coat shinier, both elbows showing neat patches.

"Miss Susan Porter."

He looked up and past Chet through the glass door which led into the small garden. On its flagstones stood a few tables under gay, colored umbrellas and potted plants ranged along its high walls.

"She was just out there, I thought. No, she went up to her room a little while ago. Pick up the house telephone, monsieur, to your right." And then, for the first time eyeing him closely, "You have an appointment with mademoiselle?"

"I do," said Chet solemnly, listening to his own voice, "but I would rather send up a little note."

The three writing desks stood side by side where they always had stood before a dark red curtain which separated the lobby from the tiny dining room.

It was hard to find words.

Chet sat in front of a thin white paper, a pointed sharp hotel pen with its tip gnawed away in his hand. Finally, slowly he wrote.

"Sue. You always believed in miracles, didn't you, and maybe that is why one happened to us. I am downstairs in the lobby, waiting."

He put the note in an envelope, absentmindedly using the wet little sponge in a crystal holder to dampen the gummed edge. The bellhop was a very young boy, inordinately proud of his uniform. He stood fixed to the ground opposite a hall mirror, so that he did not hear Chet calling. The clerk came around the desk and shook him out of his admiration of himself, and he jumped like a rabbit and rushed off into the elevator.

A few minutes later a bell on the telephone board burred loudly and the clerk again came around his desk and said:

"Mademoiselle requests that you would please ascend to 709."

Somehow he could not take the elevator. Somehow this moment should not be hastened, should be felt all the way, never to be forgotten, always to be remembered. He took the stairs. Slowly. And climbing up from floor to floor, his hand on the warm brown wood on the landing, he was able to think only of one phrase an army chaplain imprisoned with him had used constantly: Nothing is impossible.

As he came onto the seventh floor, which was also the highest, Sue stood in front of Number 709. She did not move as, now running, he came towards her. The door behind her was open and as he came closer she slowly, almost automatically moved backwards into the room; and it was Chet who, following her, closed the door, gently, definitely.

They stood, a small distance apart, a man and a woman facing each other. Behind her a door stood open, a wide French window leading to a small balcony with a low iron railing. A checked plaid rug, hastily thrown aside, lay on the floor of the balcony with a little pillow, a book, a newspaper and an apple which showed the imprint of Sue's teeth. Beyond the railing he could see across the narrow street another open window with two geranium plants and a boy sitting on the sill practicing on his violin. A lone plane could clearly be heard overhead.

They were still speechless.

Susan was very pale and her shoulders were trembling.

"Your lipstick is smeared," he said, but his voice sounded far away. "And your hair is all untidy. Ah, you never change, Sue. You haven't changed a bit."

Then she began to cry.

"Oh Chet, oh Chet. Chet. Chet."

She crossed the distance which separated them and his arms went around her and held her tight, tenderly, endlessly.

After a while Sue looked up, lifting her head a little.

"I had forgotten how tall you are," she whispered, and the tears came again, interrupted with little sobs. "You are alive. I can't believe it. You're alive. Oh Chet, I am so happy, so hap . . ."

Their lips met as they had never met before.

The noise of the plane had died away but the violin sang on.

He picked her up from the floor and carried her outside to the little balcony and put her down on the plaid on which she had rested when the bellboy had brought her his note. He sat down beside her, bracing his back against the iron railing, and took her hand in both of his. She was still trembling.

"*Sous les toits de Paris*," he said. "You and I, in Paris together. Didn't we always plan it this way?"

She could not speak just then, only sigh, and they

sat silently, their hands locked, gazing at each other in wonderment and disbelief and happiness.

"I saw you," she said suddenly. "Chet, I know I saw you! A week ago. One night at a music hall . . ." She paused. "A man sat a few tables away and I . . ." She sat up and stared at him.

He shook his head. "No," he said. "You must have made a mistake. I only came back to Paris yesterday."

"But he looked like you. He had gray hair like you. Your hair . . . oh Chet!"

"I am all right," he said. "Quite all right now. Don't cry, sweet. Don't cry. It's all over."

Her free hand gently touched his face, the scar that pulled at the corner of his lip. "What have they done to you?"

"It's all right," he said again. "It's all over." Then he smiled. "I can dye my hair and go to a plastic surgeon if you can't stand it."

"It doesn't matter," she said. "Oh Chet, no!" Her smile wavered and her eyes looked serious, "Those swine," she said. Again her eyes met his, "No," she insisted, shaking her head. "The other man's nose was crooked, too. He had gray hair and the same scar and the crooked nose and was just as thin as you. I didn't make a mistake. He moved like you, so much so that I . . . Chet, you're lying. Chet, why are you lying? You were that man at the music hall. So near. And you saw me too."

The violin had stopped. Dusk was falling. It was suddenly chilly on the little balcony.

"Let's go inside," he said, pulling her to her feet. As she turned on the light in her room he could see the pain in her eyes.

"All right," he said. "I saw you. Let me explain . . ." But then she interrupted him, resentment and hurt flaring in her voice.

"Four years, Chet! Four years. And after the first six months the news that you were missing. And from then on nothing. Nothing but all my thoughts revolving around you. All those years, months, days, nights. Can't you imagine what that would mean to a girl who loves a man?"

She threw herself on the bed and her voice changed to a whisper.

"The nights when I could not sleep. Those horrid nights when I got afraid, not about myself but about what might be happening to you. The hours when my imagination began to play tricks, and I couldn't stop it. What were they doing to you? And the days, when I set my teeth and went on working. And friends, everyone, 'Have you heard anything?' . . . The stories in the paper. The headlines! Prisoners being shot, beheaded, tortured, used for slave labor. And if you were alive you must be among them. And the days I did not know what I should wish. Maybe it would be better for you to be dead than . . ." She broke off, lowering her head, unable to understand. "And you sat there, you saw me and you were alive and safe for God knows how long a time and you wouldn't let me know. How, how could any man be so cruel?"

"Sue," he said, "nobody knows that I am alive."

Her fingers still shaking, she lit a cigarette.

He spoke rapidly, coming over to sit on the edge of the bed.

"Listen," he said. "It is important that nobody should know. Maybe it is wrong, incautious of me to have let even you know. Only I couldn't stand it any longer. I did not expect to find you in Paris."

"What do you mean 'incautious'?" she whispered. "The war is over."

"For some."

"I still don't understand!" she cried.

"There's mopping up to be done. I volunteered."

"Oh Chet," she said, "how can you? Look at you!"

"Darlingest," he said, "calm down. I'm not in half as bad a shape as I look. All this happened a long time ago. You see, in the beginning everything was swell. I came over here on a mission, accomplished it, and I guess I got a little cocky and careless. I somehow just walked into a German patrol. That's how they got me. Well, then I tried to escape, of course, and when they caught me a second time it wasn't half as pleasant."

He was making up the story as he went along and it sounded quite natural to him. She must not know the truth, under no circumstances must she know the truth.

"Oh," she sighed. "So that was it. But that doesn't answer my first question, does it, Chet?"

"No," he said, "not exactly. But you see there are still a lot of important Nazis at large. Not the big names, but they did their share of damage. One of them I know. And, as it happens, it seems possible that he might have escaped into France. As a former French prisoner of war. He also was the man who was responsible for the cruelties in my camp. That's why I volunteered for this job right away. I knew him only before . . ." and he pointed to his hair and face. "He would not recognize me now. But that's why I have assumed a Frenchman's identity . . . I am Mercier. Paul Mercier. Remember that. It is important. You, too, must forget that Chet is still alive."

Slowly she came over to where he sat and knelt down on the floor and put her head in his lap. "Revenge," she said. "Personal revenge. I can understand it. I hope the man will be caught, but haven't you done enough? Couldn't someone else . . ."

"No," he said. "I knew this particular man. We have to wipe them out. Clear out of existence if this war has not been fought for nothing; and whoever is best fitted for a certain kind of job has to do it, otherwise he hasn't done enough."

Sue gazed at Chet's long strong hands. Someone else had said almost those identical words to her last night.

"There are a few little complications connected with this," Chet said, smelling her hair and slowly bending his face and resting his chin in her curls. "Don't ask any questions. I couldn't answer them. You understand, don't you?"

"I understand," she said, and she looked at him. "And somehow I don't understand. Of course you can trust me. You know that. But you have changed, Chet. Oh Chet, you've changed. When you went . . . I mean when you left America you were only eager to get the job done and over with. Once the war was won you would have nothing to do with it. And now . . . you are going straight on into a one-man war."

"Does it surprise you?"

Slowly she shook her head. "No. No. It doesn't really. I have talked to many who feel the same way. It's just somehow that I thought you wouldn't change, you wouldn't . . ."

"I still want to build bridges across the Atlantic." He smiled, using a phrase she had coined to express his dreams of architecture.

"I still want a home in the country, a dozen children and a wife who calls herself Sue. And Sue—does Sue still want the same things? A farm up the Hudson, halfway up to Elmira so that she can be close to Mom and Dad? Three boys and two girls and old Donny for a governess? A skiing trip every second year and a beautiful chestnut mare instead of a car to ride to the post office with and to do her shopping?"

There was the shadow of a pause. And suddenly four long years in which each of them had been forced to go through life separately, alone in his joy and sorrow, fear and pain, moments of courage and cowardice, lay between them.

How could they ever be able to pick up where they had left off? So many things had happened. So many different things to each of them.

Build a bridge, Chet, thought Sue. Oh, if you only could build a bridge across the span of four years. Outside it was now completely dark.

Chet stared at the bathroom door standing ajar. Sue's dressing gown hung there. The same dressing gown for which she had saved up years ago. She had kept that. What else had she kept?

Her face did not betray what she might be thinking and he couldn't guess. What a Sue who had suffered alone and had come out of it alone would think, he could no longer tell.

The fact that neither of them had mentioned the word of love struck his consciousness. They had said they were happy, that it was a miracle but . . .

"I know," he said. "I know it is difficult. I forgot for a moment that you believed me dead. That you could no longer figure me in your plans for the future."

"Of course I do, Robert. Of course I do, Robert." He had indeed forgotten those words, had forgotten the purpose which had brought him to her.

She made no attempt to deny his implication. Instead she answered, "I had to, darling. If only because of the instinct of self-preservation. Oh Chet . . . and it was not easy."

"And it is not easy now," he said, groping for his cigarettes. "I understand. I am sorry. Don't you look so sad, darling. It is all my fault. I should have given you time to get used to . . ."

"Chet," she said, looking straight at him, her blue wide eyes clear now and calm. "The love I had for you, that kind of feeling will never change, will always be yours; but I had to bury it. And when I was all over it and could look back without going all to pieces I had learned something else, too."

"Yes?"

"That it wasn't enough," she said, crossing both hands in back of her and leaning against the cream-colored wall. "Not that it was only a puppy love, but it was a dangerous love. A love which took too much for granted from the boy next door. Neighbor children. Everything we did we did together. Part of our love was loving the memories we had together, and each other as a living manifestation of those memories."

"What do you mean?" he asked.

"I mean—oh I don't know if I can make myself quite clear; but I mean we started from where we should end after having lived an adult life together. We were not mature then and I began to wonder if it really would have lasted."

"And what has that got to do with the present situation? You haven't answered my question—you haven't answered if Sue still wants the same thing."

"Because," she said slowly, "because Sue does not know if she does." Again she grew very serious; very simply she said, "What I mean is that even if you had not been pronounced dead, darling, we would have had to meet on a new level to find out, you as well as I, if, after four years, we still wanted to share our future. That you were pronounced dead hasn't made the difference, it has only made it harder. But we would have to find out anew anyway."

She couldn't have said all this four years ago; she wouldn't have felt it.

"Maybe," he said, "maybe, but are you sure, Sue, that there is nobody else who . . ."

Sue laughed a little. "Before you went away you were the only one, Chet, always, in games, at dances. Since you went away there were a lot of others. But they did not matter. There is only one man who matters."

"The man you sat with at the music hall?"

She looked at him quickly, then nodded.

The telephone made a sudden unexpected noise. Sue

reached for it. Chet watched her, the shadow of a smile wandering over her face, the way she sat on her bed, one leg tucked under her. She was speaking French and he remembered suddenly the endless hours in his father's study when his mother had taught her language to the little blond-haired girl from next door. Sue, to show her gratitude, used to write Chet's essays in return.

She still spoke with a slight American accent.

"*Pas toujours*," she was saying, "not tonight. I will call you later perhaps. *Bien. Plus tard.*"

"That was Grandelieu," she said. "You must meet him, Chet. You and he . . . you would like each other. In some ways you are so much alike."

"You would like each other." Chet swallowed. He said, drawing out the word. "Grandelieu. There is a Grandelieu with a nasty reputation. I hope it is not the same man I mean. He . . ."

She interrupted him, laughing out loud. "I am quite sure it isn't. He is one of the most decent human beings I have ever met. People adore and respect him. He does such a lot of good. He is a doctor, was a captain in the reserve when war broke out. He fought during the few first horrible weeks then . . ."

He would not tell her that he had been to see Grandelieu under the pretext of sudden pains in his stomach.

"The man I mean," he went on slowly, casually, "is a doctor too. They say he made a lot of money during the occupation and now is covering up by spending it on the poor."

"Who says so?"

"French prisoners I was interned with. A man who knew him before it all started. Said he always was an opportunist, always after big money."

"What nonsense! Grandelieu was born rich. His father left him a vast fortune. He never needed to make money."

"For some people it doesn't matter how much they have. They always want more."

"Not Robert."

"Robert Grandelieu. That's the name. I talked to a man only yesterday. He told me . . ."

"Never mind, Chet," said Susan, anger glinting in her eyes. "People say so many things. Irresponsible things, nasty mean things, just to kill time with gossip or because they want to hurt someone's reputation for reasons of their own. I know Robert, know him well. I won't allow even you to repeat such rotten things."

"You love him? Is he the man you mentioned who means something to you?"

"Yes," she answered. "Yes, Chet, in a way I do love him. Certainly I respect him and admire him."

"I wouldn't if I were you."

Sue crossed the room and put her hand on his shoulder. "You aren't jealous, Chet, surely," she said. "Please don't. Maybe I should not have mentioned him at all to you. But we never have had any secrets."

"No, I am not jealous," Chet answered, brushing the back of her hand with his lips. "I just happen to know that what I am saying is true. I know it."

Sue stepped back. "Why, Chet?" she said. "Why, Chet?" And, after a while, glancing at him contemptuously, "Why don't you tell this to him, not to me? I dare you to repeat it to him. If you think that you are so cleverly implying that he played ball with the Germans to further his own ends or his greed, just go and repeat it to him."

"That I can't do," he told her gently. "You forget that I am on a job, that I am not at liberty to do what I might like to do." He grew abruptly silent. She mustn't repeat what he had said. Not that she would mention him under either name, he felt sure, but she might say she had heard the story. Grandelieu must not be warned. He suddenly realized angrily that all the reasons he had given himself, to make it appear necessary to see her, were false. Were neither true nor logical. If he did not want to run the risk of having Robert Grandelieu suspect something, he should never have opened his mouth.

He had wanted to see Sue. That had been it. He had wanted to see her so very much that he had not been strong enough to withstand his desire. He had been jealous, after all. It had not been simply the impulse to protect her but a selfish wish to complicate her relationship with Robert.

"Well," he said, "if you don't believe it there is no use saying anything to him."

"I wouldn't," said Sue. "He wouldn't understand and I'd never forgive myself."

No. Compared to his dreams of their first meeting after four years, everything had turned out badly. In his dreams he had done his job and had been flown over, back home across the ocean. In his dreams he had landed in New York and Sue had stood on La Guardia Field, waiting for him. The Sue of his dreams had said, "Let's get married right away, Chet. We were fools not to have risked it before you went. But now, I won't wait a moment longer." Not looked at him seriously—saying, "We would have had to meet anew anyway."

Chet grinned sourly. Dreams. Yes. Only somehow he had forgotten that he had those dreams until the moment when he had actually felt her soft and warm in his arms and had kissed her tear-wet cheeks.

Yet he had faced reality even before he had known that she was in Paris, before he had seen her sitting in the music hall with another man. The danger he was in, the goal he had set for himself. The whole situation, which even if everything turned out well, would make necessary adjustments on both sides. Hundreds and thousands of men and women like himself and Sue were coping with the problem of adjustment to normal life, to each other.

The shadow of a huge soldier of a Moroccan regiment fell across his path. Chet went on, hastening his steps.

He must forget about Sue. He must push her out of his thoughts . . . for the moment. Sue had nothing to do with what he was after. What he had to do now was to try to gather material against Grandelieu, find people who had worked with him, backtrack for anything that might be of value to him.

Grandelieu. He, too, had talked about adjustment. In a warm, clear voice he had said something about the affected and changed mentality of all the people who had lived for years under great strain, who now when everything was over and they no longer needed to make an effort, would crack. Why had Grandelieu found it necessary to lecture him? Or was he, Chet, being unnecessarily suspicious?

"You'll find people irritable, easily annoyed and quarrelsome. Or lethargic, with such deep apathy that nothing at the moment can move them. Or suspicious. Still looking for traitors, still caught in the tangle that once meant life or death. You, Mercier, too, might easily have or develop one of those symptoms. Try to rest, to rest as much as possible. Do you need money or a job? I might be able . . ."

Why this warning? Why had he offered his help to a complete stranger? Had Grandelieu suspected him of belonging to that group who were still suspicious, who still went on looking for traitors . . . ?

But Sue? Sue's instinct, which he had trusted so implicitly for almost all of his life? Sue had even refused to listen to any suggestion that Grandelieu might not be as sincere as he seemed, that he . . . Leave Sue out, Chet told himself as he went up the staircase. What does she know of the filthy background of war? How could she know? Everything pointed towards Grandelieu. He and Half Moon were identical. He had given orders in the district in which Chet had been caught. He was the man with whom Blois had worked. And the Vachon, who must have known all this, had not dared to speak of it . . . and before she could change her mind had been murdered.

He entered his room, turned on the light and sat down in front of the little writing desk. Perhaps it would be a good idea to go back to the music hall, to talk to that man at the stage door, the man whom the Vachon had said was trustworthy and whom she had called Emile.

His eyes fell on the two books he had bought several days before and placed on the ink-spotted brown leather top of the desk. Someone had been in his room, someone had been at his desk, someone had moved his things.

When he had left it he had told his old landlady that there was no need for her to go in, that he had tidied up. And he had locked the door and put the key in his pocket.

Slowly Chester pushed his hands into his pocket and brought forward a small cheap compass. It was an old habit of his, formed in his boyhood days, from the day when, for the first time, he had held a compass in his hand and his father had explained to him the miracle of a magnetic needle. The two books seemed to lie as he had put them down, only the one who had replaced them so carefully had not known that the lowest was in complete line with the magnetic pole, while the second on top lay at a point of eight degrees.

Someone, without a doubt, had moved and replaced them. There was no one in his room now. He made sure of it, looking quickly into the wide nursery closet and under the wide bed, the only two possibilities for a hiding place. He opened the window and looked out into the garden. His room was on the second floor and several little balconies ran along the back of the house. He closed the window and drew the curtains carefully, tightly.

Who was interested in him? Who had any reason to

steal secretly into his room and search it? Who, and why?

And who knew where he lived?

Again he thought of the man, the rubber-limbed, boyish-faced man who he had thought had followed him around the village, through the wood into the inn of the Lebruns and, finally followed, at least for a part of the way, the truck on which he rode back. So he had stirred up a hornets' nest after all. He had been right to go to N— and ask blunt questions.

Blois did not know, could not know anything about the prisoner of war Paul Mercier. The Lebruns knew and the Mole, and Grandelieu knew. But none of them knew his address. Only his landlady, of course. But to suspect her of anything was out of the question, absurd. She was interested only in finding out if her two daughters and a grandchild whom the Germans had kidnapped were still alive.

To the nurse in Grandelieu's office he had given the address of a hotel near the Gare du Nord. He leaned back in his chair and lighted a cigarette. Someone was getting frightened. Chet smiled.

In the quiet house he heard a clock strike two o'clock. He would not move out. He would stay where he was. He would give himself the chance to outwit whoever had been in his room. By catching him he might catch the person who was so interested in a prisoner of war called Paul Mercier.

He could see Sue sitting at one of the little marble-topped tables in front of the restaurant where he had asked her to dine with him, one of the oldest and most popular cafés of Paris. A group of soldiers at the next table was trying to flirt with her and Sue was smiling at them and their jokes.

"I am sorry," he said. "I thought women were always late."

"I would be, too," said Sue and laughed, "if I had not known a boy who could stand almost anything but being kept waiting. I remember quite well a little corner drugstore and even the lobby of the Ritz where I got the polite message of a boy who was sorry he couldn't wait any longer."

"And how angry you were. I don't think we saw each other for two whole days."

"Three," said Sue. "I couldn't quite understand what better occupation you could have than waiting for me."

"I must have been a very stupid boy."

They smiled at each other and suddenly Sue blushed.

"Oh darling, darling," she said. Then rapidly she began to speak of all sorts of things which yesterday they had forgotten to mention. His parents, his sister who had married, the way Sue had started to work at a magazine and, because several of the men had left for the war, had advanced more quickly than she would have in normal times, and how finally she had fought for this assignment.

"Human interest stories," she said. "You see, that's how I met Robert. An American major put me on to him. Robert had helped him and he told me to go and see the man who knew a lot about everything that had gone on. So I went and saw him."

Grandelieu helped an American major? Of course he would, of course he would try to make himself popular with the Americans.

"Sue," he said, speaking emphatically, "I must impress on you again that it is of the utmost importance that no one should know that I am alive. I mean, you must be very careful not to give the impression that you feel easier or . . . happier . . ."

Sue shook her head gently. "No, Paul, of course not." She looked away from him and out towards the street. "Though possibly Robert could help you in your search. It would be much easier for him to find out who would harbor a German or furnish him with false papers or help him in any other way."

Chet did not answer. To him her words held a double meaning. He was watching a thin, sick-looking dog trying to steal a piece of bread which his master held absentmindedly in his hand.

"Let's go inside and see if we can get a decent meal," he said, finishing his *apéritif*.

"Are you very hungry? It's so pretty out here."

"You should have been here years ago. Then instead of soldiers from all over the world, artists sat here. Girls and women of all ages used to come here hoping to be discovered by a famous painter, or at least to find a job as a model. They put on a terrific show. They have a grill inside and a place to dance besides the café and late at night or rather at early dawn . . ."

"Darling," interrupted Sue, "I have to confess something. I know you don't want to meet Robert. But . . ." she hesitated, put her hand on Chet's and finished quickly, "but you ought to know each other.

That's why I have asked him to come here and join us for dinner. That's why I wanted to sit outside a little longer."

Chet leaned back in alarm.

"There is no danger . . . I mean . . . you are just a man returned from three years' internment in Germany. A human interest story. Naturally I would want to talk to you. It's my job and he knows it. And Robert is always interested in anyone. Particularly in a man who has suffered a great deal."

It was all his fault. He should never have gone to see Sue. If he had been stronger, if his desire to kiss her had been weaker, if . . .

"I know you will like each other. At least you will be interested in Robert. There is no one who knows him who isn't."

And why had he added a second mistake to it all? Why hadn't he said that he had been to see Grandelieu? Grandelieu would recognize him undoubtedly as the soldier with the nervous stomach for whom he had prescribed rest. He might make a remark about it and Sue, who couldn't be told the truth, would think the obvious, that he, Chet, had first gone to see the man, to make sure it was the same she'd been with in the music hall, before he had accused him.

"I don't know what makes him late," she said. "He usually is on time even though he works so hard. I hope you aren't angry with me, Paul."

But before he could answer her she added, "Oh now I remember, it's the business about Josephine Vachon."

Josephine Vachon? Chet, who had been ready to get

up, to tell Sue that, in this case, she would have to have dinner alone with Grandelieu, sat back again.

"Vachon?"

And Sue, watching him, eager to hold him, intent on not letting him get away before Grandelieu arrived, answered willingly:

"She's, or she was, an old patient of his. That's why we went to the music hall that night. He had mentioned her to me and I wanted to interview her. The old Cancan dancer who had been such a famous member of the maquis. I thought it would make a good story."

The dog had managed to steal the piece of bread and the man was looking around stupidly, not sure if he had eaten it himself.

"And did you talk to her?"

"No," said Sue. "We sent word backstage but she had already some visitors and asked us to come up to her place a couple of days later. Well, Robert couldn't make it, and when I got there I was told she had died."

The dog was making himself as small as possible under the table, trying to avoid being seen.

"I called Robert. He was her doctor, you see. Are you listening, darling?"

"Yes, I am. What did Grandelieu say?"

"I had never known him to be at a loss for words before, but he was then. He hadn't heard. He hadn't been called in. Another doctor had signed the certificate. She was already buried when Robert got there. He talked to everyone in the house. And someone Said . . . oh, you know how people will talk in the case of a sudden death . . . that, maybe, she didn't die a natural death."

"Oh well," said Chet, "of course these are dangerous times, with people hungry and wild and unsettled."

Sue shrugged her shoulders. "Robert was terribly upset. He was very fond of her, it seems. He does not believe that her death was natural . . . I don't know. I can only guess. He doesn't talk about certain things with me. He'll say if I ask him, France is so confused right now. But anyhow, I know he wanted to find out something more about it."

Chet's face was completely impassive, no muscle stirred, his eyes fixed into space. Grandelieu again. Grandelieu and Josephine Vachon. She had been afraid. She had not dared to mention his name. And Grandelieu and Sue had known that she was having a visitor backstage. Maybe Emile, after all, was not to be trusted, never had been. And the next day before the Vachon could change her mind and talk to Chet, she had been murdered. Conveniently, another doctor had signed the death certificate so that not the slightest doubt could fall on Dr. Grandelieu who had sent Sue up and been told only by Sue. A perfect alibi. And now he was strengthening it by pretending still to be concerned about the Vachon.

Chet changed his mind. All right, he would stay and meet Grandelieu. The personal embarrassment which a remark about his visit to the office might cause did not matter any longer. He could pretend that he had dropped into the nearest doctor's office, never knowing his name, and was realizing only now that the doctor he had seen and the man he had accused were the same.

He would stay.

Either Grandelieu suspected him anyhow or, if he had been wrong in his previous assumption, then here perhaps was a chance to find some of the missing pieces he needed to expose a traitor.

They waited for half an hour more outside among the gradually emptying tables on the sidewalk before they decided to go in and order dinner.

And they finished dinner and the only good thing which came with it was a bottle of Chateau Haut-Brion. They sat and lingered over something courteously called coffee and watched the time on the big white clock over the entrance move on and on till its hands stood at eleven.

"I don't understand," said Sue. "I simply cannot understand why Robert didn't come. He could have called and let me know. I wonder what . . . why he didn't come."

Chet was wondering too.

4

Troops of soldiers were marching by when they came out of the restaurant and the old houses or both sides of the street were echoing back the melancholy, homesick tunes of soldiers everywhere.

"Try to find a cab," said Sue. "I don't care what it costs. I couldn't stand the subway just now."

Chet, who had never seen her face pale and worried with a nervous frown jumping across her round lovely forehead, gave her a long look. But he didn't say anything just then, only nodded and left her standing in the small lighted circle of the entrance. He was lucky. Two blocks further down he found a cabby whose old horse had followed the marching soldiers instinctively.

The open cab, after he had helped her climb in over the shaky two high steps, smelled as all old cabs smell, of moth balls, probably still in the pockets of the shiny coat of the driver, cheap soap with which the torn leather of the seats had been scrubbed, and the odor of horse.

The air outside was sweet and soft, streaked by moonlight and carrying all the hopes of spring. It reminded Chet of New York, of the night when, having danced in the old Plaza, Chet and Sue had counted their money, not quite sure if they had enough for a ride through Central Park. Then they had sat very close, his arm behind her shoulders, her head resting lightly against the crook of his elbow and Sue had said, "I love you, Chet. I love you so much."

Now they sat each in his corner, room enough for a third person between them, and Sue said, "It isn't at all like Robert. Something must have happened."

And instead of kissing her he could say nothing; could feel only with a stab of pain how far apart they had drifted and that their interests were no longer the same.

After a little while the cabby drew up the reins sharply. In front of them a bread line was being broken up. Angry shouts, the high screams of women who had stood for hours and the dull thuds of blackjacks.

"We'd better turn around," suggested Chet.

"No, let's try," said Sue. "I am quite used to riots by now. Every time Robert makes a speech some rowdies break in on him, trying to break up the meeting."

"Go on, *mon vieux*," the cabby told his horse and on they went, slowly, unmolested, for a few minutes. Then a crowd of men and women stopped them, gesticulating and yelling wildly something about the rich who could afford to ride in state while they were dying of starvation in the gutter.

Sue suddenly bent forward and before Chet could stop her jumped from the cab and in front of one of the men. He couldn't hear what she was saying but miraculously the racket subsided, the man touched his fingers to his bare forehead, turned and shouted something to those behind him. Sue came back. "We had better walk after all," she said. Chet pushed some bills into the cabby's hand.

"What did you say?" he asked after they walked away from the crowd and into a quiet side street.

"This is Robert's district," she answered shortly, "Guillaume just happened to recognize me." She smiled in spite of herself.

After all that noise the street seemed deeply silent, their steps echoing back towards them as they moved quickly on. Above them the full moon seemed lighter than the old-fashioned dimly lit lanterns which stood along the sidewalk at regular intervals. Then suddenly the golden square of a brilliantly lighted window fell before them onto the cobblestoned street. Sue halted her steps.

"This is where Robert lives," she said. "He is at home after all." Chet thought he heard relief in the way she inhaled the air and let it out with a deep sigh.

He had no idea where he was and in which part of Paris Grandelieu had his private quarters. He heard Sue whistle, two short, one long. Unreasonably he felt aggrieved. It was too much part of a memory he had treasured for so many lonely years: Sue standing in front of his house. Sue swinging on the garden gate, whistling their signal.

"He simply did not care to have dinner with us."

Sue didn't even answer. She continued to whistle. But no shadow showed across the window, no impatient hand threw it open, no head bent out to answer.

"He's probably asleep," said Chet.

"Nonsense," said Sue. "Not at this time of night. He usually works till dawn."

Two short, one long.

He saw her open her bag and fish around in its depths. It was a large bag, one of those monstrous affairs some women call practical. Presently Sue found what she was looking for, a key, and pushed it into the door of the small house in front of which they stood.

For a second Chet forgot that he had been betrayed, the years of internment, the death of Josephine Vachon, the job he had set for himself, the meaning of the name Grandelieu. All he felt was angry bewilderment. How dare Sue possess the key to a man's apartment? How often had she come here, whistling under a man's window? How accustomed was she to letting herself in to this man's house? All Grandelieu meant to him at this minute was the other man. The man who possessed Sue's admiration, Sue's respect, Sue's worry and care.

"Wait here for me," she said. "I'll just run up and see for myself . . ."

Behind her the door fell shut.

When she came out again Chet could not tell how long she had been. He was aflame with jealousy. But he was no longer angry with Sue. His fury was directed now solely against Grandelieu.

"He isn't there," said Sue. "He hasn't been home. The afternoon mail is on the hall table. Maybe he got a sudden call somewhere, but . . ."

"You are shaking, darling," Chet said. "Stop shaking, Sue." And he held her closely for a moment as if by physical contact he could quiet her. "Don't be so upset, darling. After all, he is a doctor, his profession . . ."

"You don't know," she whispered. "Oh, you don't know."

"What don't I know?"

"Oh don't ask me," she answered impatiently, suddenly losing control. "Something is wrong. I feel it. He only tells me what he sees fit to let me know. Come, take me home. Maybe I'll find word from him at the hotel."

But at the Atala there was no message for Sue. There had been no call.

They sat in the empty lobby, the old clerk asleep behind his desk. Somehow Chet still was unable to think clearly, to draw conclusions to fit Grandelieu's strange behavior into his tentative diagram of assumptions. He kept on watching Sue's face, alive with worry and excitement.

"You lied," he told her suddenly. "You love him very

much."

"I can't help loving him," she said absentmindedly, as if she did not realize to whom she was talking. "He's so decent." She laughed a little. "So enthusiastic," she said, and there was tenderness in her voice. "So . . ." she shrugged her shoulders in a helpless gesture. "He has enemies," she said, looking squarely at Chet. "He doesn't care. Oh, I wish I would hear from him." She got up restlessly and went across the small hall into a telephone booth.

"No answer," she said when she came back. "Still no answer. And it is almost three o'clock now."

Enemies? What kind of enemies? thought Chet, but glancing at Sue he knew that it would be of no use to question her. She was beyond answering coherently, beyond making sense. He waited for another hour, sitting silently opposite the girl he loved, watching in agony how as time went on and no call for her came in, she grew more and more desperate. When he finally left her dawn was breaking. He walked quickly along the deserted Champs-Elysées. Under the Arc de Triomphe the flame over the grave of the Unknown Soldier was burning, a sentinel was standing watch. Chet turned with the Étoile and into the Avenue de la Grande Armée. When he finally reached his house he knew for certain that at least during the last twenty-four hours nobody had followed him.

As he had promised Sue, he was back at the Atala at eleven o'clock the next morning. It was a very different Chet from the Chet of last night. This Chet had in the last few sleepless hours buried the dreams of boyhood, the dreams which helped keep him going and alive during his internment, dreams to which he had clung as someone drowning might cling to a matchstick in a threatening flood. He had idealized the girl he loved. He had forgotten that she, too, was only human and that he had no reason to be resentful, hurt and desperate, because being human she had fallen in love with someone else after he was presumably dead. It was a Chet determined to find the man who had betrayed him, to whom nothing else must matter, not even the girl he loved. It was also a Chet who had decided that all the events of last night had happened purposely, created by Robert Grandelieu, who, playing two parts, leading two lives, saw a great deal to be gained in the utter confidence of an American correspondent.

"Miss Porter isn't in," the clerk muttered; and then suddenly remembering, "Are you the gentleman who was here with her last night?"

"I am Monsieur Mercier," said Chet. "Is there a message for me?"

"That's right. Here you are." Chet was handed an envelope. When he opened it her door key fell out. Her note read: "Out on a story. Thought you might prefer to wait upstairs for me. Don't know how long I will be."

He waited on the small balcony where a few days before he had sat next to Sue holding her hand. Again, across the narrow street, the little boy was practicing his violin. But the music held no charm for him. He picked up a thin edition of a daily newspaper. Half of the world was still fighting. He thought of something one of his colonels once had said early, in the beginning. "I have no doubt that we shall be victorious. It isn't winning the war I am worried about . . . it's how we are going to win the peace." Somehow then those words had not hit home.

He heard a small noise in back of him and turned to see Sue closing the door behind her. There was something terrifyingly strange in the way she did it, gently, as gently as if she were locking the door on somebody dead.

"Sue," he said. "Sue . . . !"

He stepped into the room and found her standing next to her bed. She, who never wore a hat, was wearing a hat now, a silly high modern affair which was not at all becoming to her even though it made her look strangely elegant. She also was wearing gloves. Now, slowly, absentmindedly, she pulled them off.

"Hello, Sue," he said again.

"Oh, hello," she answered and sat down on her bed as if suddenly she was unable to stand any longer. He lighted a cigarette and placed it gently in her hand. She didn't speak, just vaguely smiled. He sat down opposite her and waited, staring at her gloves and hat, guessing by them that she had been out on official business. Then suddenly she threw up both hands to cover her face and began to cry. Chet bent forward and picked up the cigarette and crushed it.

There had been so few occasions when he could remember Sue crying. Once when her dog had died, a golden-haired spaniel called Tim; when her mother had been dangerously ill; and just a few days ago upon seeing him suddenly, unexpectedly alive. "Won't you tell me what has happened?" he asked gently. "Did you get in touch with . . . Robert?"

After a little while, drying her tears apathetically, she said in a dead voice, "Something terrible has happened, Chet . . . he . . . he has been arrested."

She began to cry again.

"Arrested?" Chet repeated quite automatically.

Stubbornly his mind refused to work. "Arrested?"

"I have been afraid of something like this," said Sue, and now that she had begun to speak her words came fast. "I warned him. I warned him to let the matter rest, not to dig into it. But no, he wouldn't, he's so stubborn. He had to find out if the Vachon was murdered or not. Oh Chet, I know you won't believe me. You are prejudiced. I don't know why or what has set you against him. But I can only repeat what I have said before—he's one of the best. He is one of the few who believe in the good and are ready to fight for it to the end. I told you he has enemies. He was essential in two or three cases where collaborators have been exposed and brought to trial. Their friends won't forgive him for that. He worked and slaved trying to help clean up the jumble of patriots and collaborators, making speeches, organizing meetings, telling people how essential it was that . . ."

Sue got up. Too excited to sit still, she began to pace the narrow distance from balcony to door, from door to balcony.

"You don't know, Chet, what is going on. You see, in the beginning the maquis needed every man ready to work with them. Elements who never should have gotten in got in that way and now are putting up a deadly fight to stay, even more than that, to assume power and throw out or destroy those who challenge them."

"You know why he has been arrested?"

Sue stopped walking. She bit her lip. "I gave my word," she said slowly, "not to mention it to anyone, at least not before it is official . . . you see, it isn't in the papers yet . . ."

There was a pause, then with a shrug of her shoulders she added:

"Intelligence with the enemy, I think is what they term treason. He's being held in Rouen."

She went out onto the balcony, turning her back to Chet.

The room in which he sat, a medium-sized French hotel room with sparse furniture, seemed to wheel around Chet, slowly first, then faster and faster like a Ferris wheel at a country fair.

Intelligence with the enemy.

Intelligence with the enemy. Grandelieu arrested, charged with Intelligence with the enemy!

He had foreseen it. Had always believed Grandelieu to have been a traitor. Once more he felt justified in having come to see Sue and having revealed that he was alive. Now she was not alone. Now she had someone to lean on.

It also meant that someone else had beaten him. That others had been suspicious of the beloved Dr. Grandelieu who treated poor people for nothing, made big speeches about how to cleanse the world of the evil elements, arranged meetings to organize his followers. All to cover up—everything designed to cover up.

And it had another meaning, too. That he, Chet, could officially return to the living, that he no longer needed to remain dead but that now that the job was finished and there was nothing left for him to do, he truly could come back to life. He and all those whom Grandelieu might have delivered over to death, torture or imprisonment had been avenged. At least one of those men who needed to be wiped out all over the world would meet justice.

So he had been right. It had been Grandelieu.

The room abruptly stopped wheeling around and with it Chet, too, was thrown off the turning Ferris wheel. He came back with a shock.

"No," he said aloud, not conscious that his lips were moving, forming words. "No. It is too easy, too perfect." Now it was he who jumped from his chair in excitement and began to pace the room. Through the open doors of the balcony the bars on the violin across the street beat on his eardrums with mathematical precision. Sober, sedate points and counterpoints. Life did not run that way. Life was not like the silver band of a river, dividing the country at its own desired width and depth, bending around the banks of rock, knowing that one day it would conquer inch by inch the defiant stone, meeting and joining up with little creeks and small rivulets to encompass them in its own innocent flow.

Life, in the twentieth century at least, was planned from its very roots to the last consequences. There couldn't be so many coincidences fitting so perfectly into each other—like the pieces of a faultlessly cut jigsaw puzzle.

Why hadn't it all happened years before? Why hadn't the Vachon died before he came back? Why hadn't Grandelieu been arrested before? Why did it all happen the day Paul Mercier began to pick up the track of the traitor?

Blois or Grandelieu? Blois or Grandelieu? Blois or Grandelieu? On the other hand there were just as many reasons for it all as there were against it. Maybe before the ultimate victory over Germany there had been no time. Or it had seemed unwise to confuse an already confused country further by bringing a charge against a man who was known by a large group as a hero.

There was no reason actually why Grandelieu should not have been the man; only, somehow, it was all too pat.

Sue came back in from the balcony. There was no trace of tears left on her face. It was quiet again.

"You must help me, Chet," she said.

He stepped back and for a second just stared at her. Then, tonelessly, he said:

"I can't, Sue. You know the reasons."

"You could if you wanted. I know you are on a job but I cannot see why that should make it impossible for you to help me."

She came across to where he stood and put both of her hands on his shoulders. "Intelligence," she said, "and Robert has been arrested because of Intelligence with the enemy. You must know people or be able to find people who know Robert, who have worked with him and through him, who could vouch for him, intervene, be witnesses for him. You can. How you manage it I don't care. I know you can do it. You must do it."

Worked with Robert and through Robert?

Worked with and through a man called Half Moon?

Chet did not answer.

"I know the Americans worked with him in the beginning," Sue said. "Robert told me a few things. Chet, you must do it. Not for my sake, but for the sake of a decent man who is being made a scapegoat."

"How can you be so sure?"

She interrupted him before he could finish. A light came into her eyes and made them seem deeper and bluer. "I am sure, Chet," she said very simply. Her eyes widened. "You would be too, Chet," she added softly. "You would be if you could question him about all those doubts you are having about him."

Now again he could hear the warm, clear voice of Dr. Grandelieu. "You will find many irritable people here, easily quarrelsome . . ." And what he had said about the reactions which surged up under the occupation . . . "distrust, still seeing traitors everywhere . . ." What if those words had held no second meaning, but had been meant sincerely; a warning, warning a homecoming man against disappointment and disillusionment.

"Maybe," Chet said. "Maybe if I could see him and talk to him he could convince me."

"And if you were convinced would you help me, would you help Robert then?"

An involuntary smile crept across Chet's face. "I

would try my best."

Sue took her hands from his shoulders and pushed them into the pockets of her jacket. "Then," she said, "then if you won't move otherwise, we must find a way for you to see him."

"Darling, darling," he said, shaking his head. Suddenly she seemed a child again, the little girl who believed the boy next door could do anything. See Robert Grandelieu. Yes, now he wanted to see him. Now, when he was completely at a loss, he wanted the chance desperately to talk to him, to form his own opinion, to put two questions to him.

And why didn't I ask him when I saw him at his office? he thought. Why? Because it was such a shock for me to find in him the man who had accompanied Sue to the music hall, because I felt so sure that it was he after what the Mole had said and after I saw the paperweight with the dedication to Half Moon.

"But who is the man who can get you a pass to see him?" he heard Sue mutter.

"And would he see a simple Paul Mercier?" he reminded her.

Sue's eyes narrowed. She sighed.

"You would have a chance but I ..."

"I don't need to see Robert to make me trust him." She gazed into space, frowning. "Maurice," she said. "Maurice! He would know what to do. If I can get Maurice to call whomever he thinks the right person and ask him to receive on his behalf his old friend Paul Mercier."

"Who is Maurice?" he asked.

"Oh, never mind." And suddenly, full of hope, she

smiled. "Chet, darling," she said, "won't you ever get used to the fact that I, too, have grown up, have met people on my own and know one or two whom you don't?" Already she was asking the hotel operator to make a connection.

"Maurice suggests you try the *Sûreté* first," Sue told Chet. Two hours later he returned.

"The prefect wasn't there," he reported. "He's never in in cases like this. I remember that from years ago. And his *Chef de Cabinet* was very sorry. Very sorry, indeed. Couldn't do anything. Of course he could if he wanted but he never wants to. The secretary was sorry. They didn't know anything about it. Grandelieu had not been arrested on their orders. As if they don't issue orders throughout the country."

Sue turned to the telephone again.

"The *Sûreté* is no good. There must be someone in Paris who has influence, who can help. And I am sure you know him, Maurice, and can get me an introduction for my friend."

Finally at three o'clock Maurice de Roland called back. Colonel Blois would see Paul at five o'clock at his home. And he was sending a letter of introduction over. Chet listened to the message impassively. Blois! So he was back in the picture again.

Blois and Grandelieu? Blois *or* Grandelieu? Blois *or* Grandelieu? It always came back to the same two men. He watched a little bird on a low branch washing its red chest with the tiny beak, turning its small head eagerly.

Chet felt for the letter in his breast pocket. There it

was all right. He stopped for a second under one of the big wide-crowned trees and lighted a cigarette. He knew he was nervous and he was intensely annoyed with himself for being so.

The villa in which Pierre Blois lived stood in a quiet dead-end street. Nothing about this street showed any mark of any of the gales of fortune which had stormed over Paris and which Paris had survived. The wars, the sieges, the revolutions, centuries ago as now. The façades of these houses were undamaged, suggesting that their owners at all times possessed enough money and influence to take care of them.

Chet, walking slowly along under the wide shady trees which studded its sidewalk, couldn't help thinking of the devastated fields he had seen; the rubble of brick and twisted iron, the landscapes of three or four different countries which all bore the scars of a mechanized all-out war. It was almost five o'clock.

The whole situation was insane. If Blois should be in the least suspicious of Paul Mercier who, in a few minutes now, was going to pretend to be the best friend of the arrested man, Blois might see fit to have him detained . . . charged with being an accomplice of Grandelieu. Then he would be forced to reveal his true identity, would lose any chance of finding out the truth and on top of everything would create a fine mess. Anyone would wonder why an American officer should visit a prominent Frenchman under an assumed name.

"But remember you are strictly on your own," his colonel had said. Chet threw the half-smoked cigarette away. He set his jaw. For a moment he felt violently angry with himself. He should never have allowed Sue to sway him. Then he remembered that he wasn't here for Sue's sake alone but in his own Interests as well. He had to take every chance to find out the truth.

He crossed the street and a moment later rang the bell at Number 3. It seemed to be one of those which set several other bells swinging, for he could hear a cascade of harmonious notes faintly echoing inside the house. After a pause which seemed endless to Chet an elderly uniformed servant opened the door.

The hall into which he stepped was at the street level and almost dark.

"Colonel Blois is expecting me," he said, handing his letter to the servant who bowed in acknowledgment and at once disappeared, leaving Chet waiting. When his eyes grew used to the darkness he saw that the light was dim because it fell through two large stained-glass windows which presented scenes from the Bible. There was a wide staircase swinging up in a graceful curve to the second floor. At the foot of the stairs stood an atrocity of a huge stuffed white bear holding a tray for letters or *cartes de visite* in its unnaturally bent left claw. Chet stepped nearer and read the small plaque.

It was apparently a present to Pierre Blois from a proud hunter.

"The colonel will receive you now. Will you please follow me?" a voice said behind him.

The room to which he was shown was very large and exquisitely furnished with antique pieces, yet its atmosphere was cold in spite of all its beauty.

At the far end between two French windows opening into a garden. Pierre Blois sat behind a Louis XV library table. He was writing. As Chet entered he looked up for a second, incuriously but politely.

"Please make yourself comfortable. I'll be at your disposal in a minute."

There was the voice again, the sober voice which four years ago had said, "Any questions? *Bonne chance, mon capitaine!*"

Blois's attitude, his concentration on whatever he was writing, was obviously a pretense. Chet knew he was being watched. He could tell it by the way Blois's hand held the pen, moved it across the sheet of white paper, the way his hand was tilted.

Chet sat down in an embroidered chair. It was only natural that Blois should be inquisitive if the Comte de Roland had repeated to him what Sue had said. Paul Mercier . . . a close friend of Grandelieu. Now he, too, pretended not to watch the colonel. To all appearances he was staring out of the window, singularly interested in the formation of clouds he could see rising across the chimneys of the other houses. Just then Blois looked up, feeling safe, and for a moment the glance of the two men crossed, then, quickly, each of them looked away, both courteously ignoring the other's curiosity.

Then there was nothing but the slight scratch of a pen hurrying over paper. Quite unexpectedly Blois pushed his chair back, got up and came around his desk and toward Chet.

That's a man who likes to surprise the other fellow, Chet thought as he rose, too. The two men stood facing each other, a separation of only two feet between them. Chet could see Blois's eyes again. Cold, arrogant eyes under the wide big forehead.

He'll never help me, he thought.

Again as a surprise to him Blois's hand came forward to rest on Chet's arm.

"Let's sit down over there in the corner where we'll be more comfortable," said the cold, polite voice. Blois pointed across the room to a small love seat and a few deep chairs around a smoking table. As he sat down, he said, "Well, Mr. Mercier, what is it I can do for you? My friend the Comte de Roland tells me that you were a prisoner of war for more than three years and have only recently got back to our country. How long have you been here?"

Chet remembered what he had seen and heard about other prisoners of war: how demanding their behavior was; and he decided not to be humble but to take the advantage of a man who has suffered. It would suit his purpose better.

"About two weeks, *mon colonel*."

"So little as that," said Blois and he clicked his tongue a little against the back of his upper teeth. "Well, I hope you found your relatives and friends . . ."

"I have no relatives in Paris," said Chet. He waited for further questions but Blois with courtesy only said, "Then you must feel very lonely. It is difficult to get used to such changed conditions in Paris. I understand. Well, your friends here will certainly do everything they can for you."

"As far as they are able to, certainly . . ." Chet said quickly, his eyes fixed on Blois's face.

"And your friends have advised you to see me? It's almost impossible to help everyone. Nevertheless I, or we, all of us, try to do our best to be of help to the uprooted. Jobs . . . ?"

Another voice, a gruff sullen voice, seemed to say, "We have no jobs here. Get out." So clearly did Chet imagine he heard the Mole's voice that he looked up to the painted, arched ceiling across which seventeenth-century angels sported with huge silver fish and golden stars. The Mole down in the village of N— at the Blois estate had jumped to the same conclusion. After all, it was a very natural assumption in times like these.

"*Mon colonel*," he said, "I didn't come to ask a favor of you on my behalf. I came to ask your help to make it possible for me to see a friend who has been arrested."

He saw Blois straighten up a little, then cross his long legs, staring down along the shiny boots.

"Did you tell the Comte de Roland the true reason for which you wanted to see me?"

"No, of course not, *mon colonel*."

"Then why, monsieur, do you come to me? I am no official. If your friend, monsieur, is innocent then he'll be released shortly. If not . . ." and he shrugged his shoulders.

"You must see him for yourself, you must talk to him, then you will be convinced that Robert is not guilty," Sue had cried.

"This," said Chet, "is a very special case. I never expected you would help me if my friend is guilty but I did hope that you would be willing to help find the truth."

"The truth, of course," said Blois. "But why do you mistrust our courts? What is it your friend is accused of?"

Chet made his decision quickly. He pretended not to have heard Blois's question. He said casually, his voice flat:

"You know him, *mon colonel*. Dr. Robert Grandelieu."

Blois's face registered open surprise. His eyebrows went up and for a second his mouth fell apart, showing a row of very small, even white teeth.

"Grandelieu," he repeated. "That is strange, indeed." He turned his head. "Yes, I do know him slightly."

Chet forced himself to smile. "Maybe I am making a mistake but I remember Grandelieu telling me that he was working with London in the early days and I assumed that you knew him."

Now Blois's face was a blank, even the pupils of his eyes remained fixed.

"That's what he said? I see. Well, tell me why he has been arrested and what he is charged with."

Chet sighed, half intentionally, half unconsciously.

"I don't know," he said. "Nobody seems to know. That is what worries me. That is why I came to ask you to help me clear this up."

"And what exactly do you want me to do?"

The voice was very cold now. The voice in the London office saying coldly, "Any questions?"

"I want to see him. He was arrested in Rouen. I want a pass to see him there."

"And may I ask, monsieur, what your personal interest is in this case?"

Chet stood up and so did Blois. Again they were facing each other. Then Chet said, "*Mon colonel*, he is my friend and I want to help him. We are living in a time in which it is difficult to be sure of the truth. All of us, I believe, must feel it our duty to make sure that justice is done. Even the very wisest and best judges can err, can make a mistake on false evidence . . ." He paused and then added matter-of-factly, "Greater and more important people than Grandelieu have been victimized."

Again the room was frighteningly silent. Any moment now, feared Chet, feeling Blois's eyes still resting on his face, he will tell me, "But I know you, don't I? Aren't you Captain Burton?"

Instead Blois said, "And you, monsieur, are convinced that Grandelieu is innocent of any wrongdoing?"

"I swear he is not guilty," Sue had said. "Chet, I know him. He is one of the best . . ."

"I find it difficult to believe otherwise, *mon colonel*."

"And why don't you see the prefect? He is the proper person to see."

"The prefect is away," said Chet.

A faint smile ran like lightning along Blois's mouth. But he was silent. He began pacing the room, then turning towards Chet again he said:

"I'll think it over. Come back about nine o'clock and I will let you know if and how I may be able to help you."

Outside the street was the same. Everything was the same. Nothing had been solved. No answer had been given.

Blois or Grandelieu? Blois or Grandelieu? It still was the same question.

Sue was certain of Grandelieu, certain that he was innocent. But if Grandelieu was innocent then Blois was the man. And it still seemed impossible. There was nothing, not the slightest twig to which he could tie his suspicions as far as the colonel was concerned. He had not trusted Chet, but it would have been just as strange to trust a complete unknown who in some way was involved in the Grandelieu affair. Would he get him the permission? Chet knew that a man like Blois had connections, was powerful, could unquestionably do so if he wanted to. But even if he refused to have anything to do with the whole matter, it would only be natural. Why should he stick out his neck if Grandelieu was guilty?

No, there was nothing Chet could reproach Blois for. Nothing which helped him to agree with Sue. Only one little remark had been odd.

"Grandelieu. Yes, I do know him slightly."

Slightly? "To Half Moon, in memory, P.B."

They had worked together. That much was certain. Worked together in matters of life and death. Even though they might in the beginning not have known each other's true identity, more than a year had passed in which they could be revealed without danger. Slightly?

Personally they might have known each other slightly, but the knowledge of their reputations could not have been a slight one. But then again why should Blois admit anything to a complete stranger? How could Blois know what he, Paul Mercier, might really want? If he had been careful and noncommittal that, too, was only the normal attitude of a wise and powerful man.

It was almost dark when Chet came back. The same servant who had admitted him a few hours before let him in. Again Chet stood in the hall, now brilliantly lighted, opposite the atrocious white bear which in a fantastic way seemed to bare its terrific teeth at him. From behind the door of the room where he had met Blois in the afternoon came voices. Another servant whom he hadn't seen before was hurrying through the hall, disappearing into the corridor at its left, and the clatter of dishes from a pantry could be heard.

In the corridor another door opened and for a second Chet could see steps leading up behind it. A young man in uniform came through it and towards Chet.

"The colonel asked me to excuse him. He has guests and . . ." So he refused, thought Chet. But the young man went on, speaking slowly and meticulously. "The colonel is very happy to have been able to arrange everything for you." He pulled out a letter and handed it to Chet. It was addressed to the director of the prison in Rouen . . . advising him to allow the bearer to see the prisoner, Robert Grandelieu.

Chet stared at it, hardly believing his eyes.

"Will you please express my sincere gratitude to the colonel?"

"There is a car going to Rouen tonight," said the young man with his automatic gestures and his meticulous voice, "to fetch some friends of the colonel. If you care to, you can go with it. It should be here any moment."

Chet jumped at the offer. Again he asked the young man to thank Blois for him. Just then he heard a car pull up at the curb and the young man went out and came back, saying, "The chauffeur has already had his instructions. Well, good luck. *Bonne chance.*"

Between two lanterns stood a long black car, a town limousine with an open space for the driver, a type of car which had been popular in Europe before the war. The chauffeur was sitting behind his wheel. The motor was running.

"Will you please stop at a telephone booth before we get out of Paris?" Chet said, jumping into the car and slamming the door behind him. He saw the man nod and leaned back into his seat, sighing deeply with relief. What he hadn't expected was going to happen. In a few hours more he would see Robert Grandelieu.

Then the realization of what this all meant struck him. All the doubts he had had about Blois fell away like a house of cards. So it was true what his colonel and everyone else had been saying of Blois, that he was a decent man beyond all doubt. Again Blois had proved it, had stuck his neck out in a touchy matter, had made an attempt to help Grandelieu. It also meant that he could eliminate Blois. Again all suspicions centered around Grandelieu. No longer Blois or Grandelieu, only Grandelieu. But then there was Sue swearing that Grandelieu . . . Could the girl he loved love a traitor? Suddenly he remembered something he had forgotten ever since he had returned from the little village of N—, his own colonel's words:

"Blois is considered a hero and it is expected that he

will be appointed to a high office in the government. The other—I don't remember his name if we ever knew it, but I do remember that we had no reason ever to distrust him. The only possibility I can see now is that an unknown third somehow managed to get hold of the secret."

He had forgotten that possibility.

Would Robert Grandelieu, if he actually were innocent, know who this possible third could have been?

The car came to a stop in a dark suburban street Chet had not noticed that they had already reached the outskirts of Paris. A dim light hung over the entrance of a bistro. He went in quickly, found the booth and dialed Sue's number.

"Everything is all right," he told her. "I've got the permission, I am . . ." Then with a sharp click the connection was interrupted. He tried twice again, went out into the room to look for another telephone and saw the chauffeur leaning against the bar, drinking a glass of beer. He didn't look like a man who would customarily represent the chauffeur of powerful and rich people. He was of sturdy and broad build and his face was hard, mean and tough. His voice was sullen, rough and uneducated as he asked now, "Trouble with the phone, monsieur?"

Had he been watching him through the glass door of the booth? thought Chet. And why should he watch him? He didn't like the man's face or his voice.

The owner of the bistro, a big man with bare tattooed arms and a torn apron across his belly, went into the booth, trying to fix the connection, and came back out, shaking his head.

"The war," he said. "There is still something wrong with the lines. Sorry."

Chet stood hesitantly, then shrugged his shoulders. Anyhow Sue knew that he had the pass. He would be back sometime during the following day and she would guess that he had probably tried to find transportation to Rouen immediately.

"Well, monsieur," said the chauffeur, "any time you are ready, I am."

"I am ready," said Chet. He thought he saw the chauffeur smirk.

5

I didn't like the man's face, thought Chet, staring through the tonneau window, and now I don't like his back either. But, he thought, listening to the even hum of the engine, he seems to be a good driver. He leaned back in his seat pulling from his pocket the letter Blois's secretary had handed him. A small piece of paper. Nothing but a small piece of paper and yet on it might depend entire futures. Grandelieu's, Sue's, mine, and perhaps, perhaps that of still another person. He folded it carefully and then, instead of putting it back into his hip pocket, he opened the shirt buttons under his tie. From his throat, across his chest, on a thin cord hung the little leather pouch in which he carried large bills and an identification tag.

The highway was almost empty of traffic, bumpy from the many heavy loads which had rolled across it during the past years, lorries and caissons and big guns and tanks; but still the car was speeding.

They should make Rouen in about three or four hours depending on the road and how many bomb craters remained still unrepaired or under reconstruction. Chet could remember Rouen, the little old town on the shores of the Seine where Corneille and Flaubert had been born and where Jeanne d'Arc in the fifteenth century had died in the leaping flames. He had been in Rouen seven years before, on a walking trip through Normandy. Why in the world had Robert Grandelieu been imprisoned there? Why had he been arrested there instead of Paris and how and why should a busy doctor go to Rouen? He remembered Sue's lovely face with the nervous frown jumping between her eyebrows, her worried voice: "It's that Vachon business. I told him to let it rest but he wants to find out."

Had Robert Grandelieu gone to Rouen because some link connected Josephine Vachon with that city? And what kind of link? Something Grandelieu wanted to cover up for his own sake or something connected with her death? And there, back he was again at the same old question. Was Grandelieu the man who had betrayed him, the man to blame for the murder of the old Cancan dancer, or . . . ? If it were not for Sue and her faith in him nothing had happened which refuted Chet's suspicions. Except the rebellious feeling he had had after the first reaction on hearing about Grandelieu's arrest: that somehow it fitted in too well, too neatly, too smoothly.

Smoothly? thought Chet. He sat up with a start.

"Smoothly," he said in a half whisper to himself. If he was judging by the way affairs ran, then most certainly the whole affair with Colonel Blois had gone surprisingly smoothly.

Surprising, rather, that Blois had found time to see him immediately on the very day Sue's friend had asked him to give an interview to Paul Mercier. Not the next day, nor the following day, but the very same afternoon. Blois, the great man, the busy man, finding time for an unknown. And the long time he had given him? Why hadn't he asked how Paul Mercier, back in France after three years and in a city where he had not lived before, could possibly know of Grandelieu's arrest when it had been kept silent and out of the papers? Had Blois known about the arrest? Was that why he hadn't asked? He had been surprised. But about what? About the fact Grandelieu had been arrested or that Paul Mercier knew about it?

They passed through the town of Vernon and came out onto the highway again. There was hardly any moonlight. Once in a while the clouds would scatter and, in such moments, Chet could see the broad ribbon of the Seine slipping along at their left.

At nine o'clock the pass had been there. Which meant that Blois must have gone to considerable trouble at a time during which all offices were closed. Even Sue hadn't hoped for anything like a pass as quickly as that.

"We'll be lucky if he'll give you a personal note to the prefect or tell you to come back tomorrow," Sue had said before he had left her at eight.

But not only had the permission been granted and

ready but also Blois had been considerate enough to think of transportation for him.

Was it a mere coincidence that he was sending an automobile to fetch some friends from Rouen? Mere kindly concern for an unimportant Paul Mercier to help him see a friend, a friend whom Blois had said he himself knew only—slightly? Grandelieu or Blois? Blois or Grandelieu? Grandelieu or Blois, the wheels hitting the cement of the road seemed to swish. The old dilemma again. Nothing was solved.

"Bonne chance," the secretary had wished him, "Good luck. *Bonne chance."* And again the wheels took the words, rolling them along with their speed. *Bonne chance. Bonne chance. Bonne chance.*

Four years ago in the London office Colonel Blois had extended his hand to him, wishing him *"Bonne chance"*; and he had hardly untangled his parachute there on the meadow belonging to the Blois estate in N— when the Germans had stepped forward to seize him.

The Mole came back into Chet's thought; the man chopping wood behind the stone fence. From then on he had been followed. Why not before? Why not after he had visited the Vachon and later when he had discovered her murder? Why only after he had revealed to several people down in N— that he had known the American flier who had been caught in their village and knew he had been betrayed?

Chet felt perspiration breaking out over his eyes. He reached for his handkerchief and wiped his forehead. Sue that afternoon had put some Eau de Cologne on the linen and now the smell of lavender came sharp and refreshing into his nostrils.

It was impossible that Blois had recognized him as Chester Burton. If the girl who had known him all his life hadn't known him, most certainly a man who had seen him only once for a few minutes, and who must think him dead, wouldn't be suspicious.

But, he told himself, I have been followed only since I left N—. There I talked to a man in Blois's service, the Mole. Could the Mole have notified his employer about a strange man asking a lot of questions about a betrayed American officer who had been shot against Pierre Blois's garden wall? Assuming that Blois had been responsible . . . then to him the returned prisoner of war, Paul Mercier, possibly would be a dangerous witness.

Had the trail he had followed, the trail which led so pointedly to Dr. Robert Grandelieu, been laid intentionally? Or had it been a mere coincidence?

And what if Sue was right? If Grandelieu actually was innocent? Why then had he been arrested just at the time when Paul Mercier came on the scene? What was behind Grandelieu's surprising arrest? Because in some way or other Grandelieu, like the Vachon, knew too much, too much that was dangerous? To whom?

Nonsense, Chet told himself. Your imagination is running away with you. After all Blois gave you the pass, made it possible for you to go and see and speak with Grandelieu. He would never have done that if he had anything to fear.

Suddenly he was taut. Suddenly the wheels' ominous song began again. *Bonne chance, bonne chance, bonne chance.*

Think clearly now, Chet. How would you talk and behave if you wanted to win a man's confidence for a certain purpose? Wouldn't you behave as Pierre Blois had, for then you would have a chance to . . .

He leaned forward. The chauffeur did not look like a chauffeur. . . . I, he said to himself, am riding in Pierre Blois's car in a dark night on an empty highway. If . . . His right hand groped for the pistol in his pocket. If . . . he thought. He saw the chauffeur move the mirror above the wheel; then, lighting a cigarette, Chet leaned back in his corner, half closing his eyes.

The car sped on evenly. And Chet, tense, was watching the man's broad back through the window. A few minutes passed before he saw the right arm of the man fall back from the wheel, resting casually on the seat. He bent forward again, crouching low, watching the man's right hand. Slowly, cautiously it moved, to be laid gently on the door handle. Chet's left hand shot forward, clutching the handle of the door on the opposite side, turning it.

In the beam of the headlights he could see a curve ahead, sharp, hairpin . . . then slowly the man moving more to the right, shifting his body as if tired. For a second Chet could see the lighted dashboard, no longer hidden by the broad back. There was the curve, into which they went, the car gaining speed and then suddenly, instead of pulling out, hurtling for the river.

He didn't see the chauffeur jump from the speeding car, but he thought he saw him fall out to the right towards the highway; the next moment Chet was diving away from the falling car, which had jumped the steep embankment into the broad river. He hit the water a few feet away a second before the car did. It sank at once, shooting a fountain of water into the air which fell hard and painfully on him as he came up, forcing him down again. He rose once more, the air stabbing his lungs, before he dived of his own volition.

The water was icy cold and Chet was counting one, two, three. After ten strokes his lungs gave out and he had to come up. He felt a cramp in his left leg knotting his muscles, sharp as a knife. He turned with great effort onto his back, floating limply, letting the current carry him. Above him the sky was clouded. He can't possibly see me, he thought. He jumped out when the car was going at great speed. God knows where the momentum threw him. He decided that it was safe to swim. The cramp still bore into his leg like an animal digging its teeth in.

The current was not very strong but the river was wide and Chet, lifting his head to try to get his bearings and to measure the distance to the shore, suddenly felt weak. It seemed so far away. Three years of slave labor, insufficient food, constant ill-treatment, suddenly exacted their toll on him, at this moment when he most needed his strength. He could hear his heart hammer; he thought his ribs would burst, snapping like matches. Then his right leg grew stiff, paralyzed by the chill of the water. His clothes and boots, waterlogged, began to drag him under.

Life all of a sudden seemed terribly futile. Innocent people could be framed and stuck in prisons while the rats were busy getting themselves a place in the sun.

A man not quite thirty years old came back with the strength of a baby. A man came back from hell to find his girl in love with someone else. A brave old woman who had risked her life a hundred times to help her country could be murdered and no one even bothered.

Resignation, depression and pain almost finished him. Then, from out of nowhere, the instinct for self-preservation made him part the water again automatically. Hell, to drown like a cat here in a French river was not what he had fought for.

Miraculously he felt unexpected ground under his feet. He began to wade, the water still reaching up to his chin. His outstretched hands felt the bank rising steep and high above him. No tree roots, no branch, nothing, to help him drag himself up. Still standing in the river, he leaned his face against the bank. The smell of the soil came sweetly to him, damp and warm. He breathed deeply. He hung there for a while, feeling his heart calm down while his legs were weightless, floating under him. There was no sound except his own deep breathing, the swirl of the river and somewhere overhead a slight wind sighing through the night. Then he straightened himself and, holding on to the shore, he moved along trying to find a place to climb up. Twenty yards further on he could make out the dim outlines of something which seemed like a landing stage. He touched two poles, shaky and moldy. Between them ran a length of boards. Some of them were broken, some simply no longer there. He pulled himself up and by carefully hunching forward he came to a staircase hewn into the embankment. The landing was missing but the stairs led in soft curves up to road level and the highway. There trees stood, apple trees in bloom. Across the highway he could see the cottage to which, apparently, the staircase and landing stage belonged. It was dark. But next to it he saw a light. Dim, shining through a high Gothic window frame. A church. A little church amidst blooming apple trees.

Chet stumbled forward, not quite conscious of what he was doing but magnetically drawn by the light. As he came closer he could hear music and when he opened the door the full peal of an organ met him. In the shadow a priest sat playing with devotion. A Bach fugue. Chet could not see him clearly; he only saw the long thin candles at either side of a primitively carved and painted altar. He slipped into one of the crude benches, he let his head sink forward. He felt he wanted to cry, to say grace and, somehow, defiantly to scream. He did none of these. He fainted.

When he came to he was lying on a cot. Above him the ceiling was bare and white, as were the walls. A candle was burning on a stool next to his cot and the gigantic shadow of a man sitting near him flickered across the opposite wall. A deep voice said, "Drink this, my son." A large rough hand, its nails grimy and broken, with calluses under the fingertips, held a glass to his mouth.

"It's hot cider. It's good for you. Besides it's the only thing I can offer you."

Chet lifted himself on one arm and saw that he was naked, covered by two rough gray blankets. He reached automatically for the leather pouch around his neck. It was gone.

"Don't worry," said the priest. "I hung up your clothes and here is what you're looking for. I haven't opened it."

Chet clutched the little bag, then opened it. The Pass, neatly folded, was still there inside the watertight lining. He lay back and now for the first time looked directly at his host. The priest was a large man with a bald head, his eyes were bloodshot, skin tanned, his chin clean-shaven.

"Where am I? And how far is it to Rouen?" Chet asked.

"You are in a little village, eleven miles from Rouen, at St. Adrien." Chet lay back again on his arm, drinking the hot liquid slowly, gratefully.

"I was tired," he said. "I had been walking all day. I don't know how many miles. I sat down to rest. In my sleep I must have fallen into the river, I guess. I didn't realize how steep the embankment was."

The priest smiled at him. "You are very weak, my son," he said. "Rest. Spend the night here and tomorrow you can tell me anything you like."

He watched the priest undress, hang up his soutane on the nail under which his wide round hat was swaying gently. He saw him go out, heard the screech of a pump in the courtyard, saw him come back, carrying a glass of water and a piece of homemade bread.

"We are a very poor community here," he said conversationally. "There is only one window left in the church; all the others were broken by the war; and the organ needs tuning. And we need more Bibles. But God has brought us safely through." He knelt and began to pray. Then making the sign of the cross over Chet, he smiled again and sank down on a cot standing opposite.

"Good night, my son, and may God bless you whoever you are." He blew out the candle. Then there was nothing but darkness, the slight snoring of the poor village priest and, once in a while, the whimsical noise of a goat dreaming aloud in her sleep in the shed back of the priest's cottage.

It was in this dark, shabby room that Chet reluctantly faced a fact which he had been unconsciously avoiding. Now, when it was obvious Blois had tried to murder him, to murder Paul Mercier as once he had tried to murder Chester Burton . . . a car overturning at a sharp curve, plunging into the wide deep river . . . there was no doubt in Chet's mind that Robert Grandelieu was innocent.

Sue had been right.

Sue.

How strange life was, how cruel. That of the millions of men in the world he should have been chosen to help the only man in that same world who was taking what had belonged to him. Sue.

Why? he thought. Why I?

There had been other nights when unable to sleep in the stench of the barracks, too exhausted even to rest, he had asked the same question. Why I?

On one of those nights another man who could not sleep had asked into the pain-filled quiet:

"I sometimes wonder what makes a man kill . . . I mean in war, shoot and kill other men who haven't done anything, who are just obeying orders the same way I am. I used to think that I could never stick a bayonet into another man. Even in training when I had to ram it into the dummy I felt sick. And then I went and did it. I wonder why?"

"Why?" someone else had answered. "I felt the same as you did. I thought I would rather die myself than do it. Then why didn't I? Shall I tell you, bud? Because you know if you don't, the boy at your left or the boy at your right or the boy behind you will get killed. That's why we all do it."

Sleep, soft and sweet, came to Chet quite unexpectedly. He tried to fight it off. Sue, he thought, Sue . . .

Dawn was breaking when he woke.

The priest was still snoring. Chet reached for the glass of water which he had not drunk the night before. It was stale but he drank it thirstily and ate the bread. He felt rested and the night before seemed unreal, a wild nightmare. Yet he knew it was true and he knew also that he had no time to lose, that he must get to Rouen as quickly as possible. And that, above all, no one must know that Paul Mercier hadn't drowned in the Seine.

He almost laughed then. There he was stretching in the early morning, very much alive, very much set on what he had to do, and yet twice dead. Once shot by the Germans, the second time drowned by a Frenchman. And the same man had murdered the same man twice.

No, he mustn't be seen. Under no circumstances. Pierre Blois must believe, as he had believed, that

Chester Burton was dead, that Paul Mercier had died. Sue, he thought again. He hoped that she wouldn't hear anything. But then there was little possibility. A car had overturned, no one would know who its passengers were. And if they ever found the car, the bodies would be gone, apparently freed somehow and carried away by the current.

His glance wandered around the bare room. It fastened on the soutane and the wide-rimmed hat hanging on the nail. Chet closed his eyes quickly, not really wanting to think what he was thinking. Then he opened them again. What a perfect disguise. He reached into his pouch, took out a large bill and noiselessly placed it on the stool near the candle. There was a pad and a pencil hanging under the soutane when he took it off its nail. He wrote a few lines, carefully printing the words.

I HOPE YOU WILL FORGIVE ME. I WILL RETURN YOUR PROPERTY AS SOON AS POSSIBLE. MINE ARE STILL WET AND I HAVE TO MOVE ON. IN THE MEANTIME HAVE THE WINDOWS AND THE ORGAN FIXED AND DO WITH THE REST WHATEVER YOU THINK BEST. THANK YOU, FATHER.

He slipped out on tiptoe. In the kitchen he found his underwear dry, his suit as he had expected, still sodden. A few minutes later he was walking along the highway in the direction of Rouen.

The prison warden examined the pass carefully

when Chet presented it to him in his office. He pushed his rimless glasses up onto his forehead, then lowered them again over his eyes. Finally he nodded, glanced at Chet and nodded again. Then he pressed the bell. To the entering guard he said in his high thin voice:

"Take the father to the prisoner Grandelieu."

It was an old-fashioned building with none of the modern equipment of the twentieth century. The walls were thick, about three feet through, and the stone was sweating. Chet went through long corridors, following the guard who was wearing loose slippers and complained as they walked about the shoe shortage. From behind the cells on both sides of the corridor came voices. Once the guard shrugged.

"We simply have no room for any more," he said. "One would think the Germans were still here. It all goes so slowly. Half of them should be released and aren't yet and still others keep coming. I think most of them steal only to get in here so that at least they will get something to eat every day and have a place to sleep."

But, nevertheless, Robert Grandelieu was alone in his cell.

Chet saw a tall man leaning against the barred window, his back to the door.

"Grandelieu," the guard called. "Someone to see you." He turned to Chet. "You call when you want me." He went out, locking the door behind him, but adjusted the small window in the frame so that he could watch through it from the corridor. Apparently in Chet's special permission there were no restrictions made as to time or conditions under which he could see the prisoner. Pierre Blois, Chet reminded himself, had never expected the bearer to reach his destination.

Robert Grandelieu still stood motionless, as if he had grown deaf and dumb. Chet wondered what they had done to Grandelieu to make him so incurious, so indifferent.

He said gently, "Dr. Grandelieu, won't you turn around to see who I am?"

Slowly Robert turned. His face was white as if drained of all blood. His dark eyes seemed enormous. His pale lips were set in a hard small line of determination. He looked at Chet for a moment then, shrugging his shoulders, he turned back again to stare out between the bars.

"I am your friend," said Chet, listening to his own words which were forced by his sympathy. "You can trust me."

There was no answer and Chet, moving closer to the rigid lonely figure at the window, lowered his voice:

"Sue sent me."

Again there was no answer.

"Sue sent me," Chet said again.

Without turning Grandelieu said, "I don't know whom you mean." The only thing alive about the man, it seemed to Chet, was his voice. Though strained, it still held its natural warmth.

Chet was almost whispering now, glancing over his shoulder to see if the guard was listening. "Susan Porter."

"I don't know anyone by that name."

Chet realized abruptly that Grandelieu would never admit to anyone that he knew the girl they both loved.

At least, not to anyone he didn't trust completely . . . that he wanted to protect her, to keep her out of any possible danger.

"Nevertheless," he replied, "she and I are perhaps the only people in the world who can help you now. You see, no one knows that you have been arrested. It hasn't been in the papers and it was Sue who found out that you were in prison in Rouen."

Still Grandelieu seemed to guard against a trap. He remained silent. Then, after a while, he asked:

"Who are you?"

"Turn around and look at me."

Grandelieu did not alter his position. "I saw you and I have never seen you before."

"Look again," said Chet. "I thought you had a better memory. I came to you as a patient."

"A doctor sees many patients. I used to see as many as a hundred a day. Sometimes more." But he turned and faced Chet.

"Only a few days ago . . ." Chet reminded him. Into Grandelieu's eyes came a light of recognition, his lips opened, then he sighed and turned around again.

"Many people go to a doctor," he said, shrugging his shoulders.

"Tell me," said Chet, "what can I do to help you? Haven't you any influential friends?"

"I wouldn't know."

Chet moved a couple of steps forward. Now he stood directly beside Grandelieu. He had not planned his next move but Robert Grandelieu was behaving as he, Chet, would have behaved in a similar situation. He knew he himself would not volunteer any information.

"Half Moon," he whispered. "Half Moon!" He saw Grandelieu start with surprise, the quick movement of his hands, then he stood rigid again. Chet reminded himself that anyone entering Grandelieu's office could pick up the name. He had to shock Grandelieu into a response.

"Josephine Vachon was murdered," he said. "I saw her that day . . . hanging in her own kitchen . . . I had an appointment with her."

Robert Grandelieu swung around, fastening his burning eyes on Chet. For a moment Chet thought that Grandelieu had decided to drop his caution. Then he discovered that he had erred for Robert put no question concerning the Vachon. Instead he asked again:

"Who are you?"

"I told you, someone you can trust."

He had never intended to reveal his true identity, but now he saw that this man would never speak. Because he was not afraid for himself but afraid of involving anyone connected with him. This man, Chet was sure, was ready to die rather than cause the death of one more person if he could help it. Somehow Chet had expected Grandelieu to behave differently, to jump at a chance to talk, to assure him that he was innocent, imploring him to take steps, to appeal to his friends.

"Grandelieu," he said, "maybe you remember one night recently when you went with Sue to a music hall in Paris. You wanted her to meet Josephine Vachon. Well, she didn't see you because she had a visitor. I was the visitor that evening. You noticed that

Sue suddenly was depressed and when you questioned her, she indicated a man nearby and asked you not to look right then. She said that the man sitting there somehow reminded her of someone she had loved all her life . . . and who was dead. *Supposedly* dead."

Grandelieu turned so violently that he almost knocked Chet against the wall.

"My God!" he said. "My God! I cannot believe it. My God." He stared at Chet. Chet shook his head.

"I've changed," he said, "but, nevertheless, I landed three years ago at N— only . . ."

Robert straightened and spoke with authority. "You remember the date?"

"The fourteenth of May."

"Who was the man in London who put you onto Half Moon?"

"Peter Smith . . . at least that's what he called himself then."

"And I thought . . ."

Robert reached out his hand to take Chet's. "They told me you had been shot."

"Do you know what went wrong?"

"No." Robert shook his head. "The orders came over by carrier pigeon. I had rented a house in the country to be less obvious. Ten miles from N—, Sagitta, an American, would land at two o'clock in the morning on the meadow of the Blois estate. I was to get everything ready for him. We had plenty of time, it was all organized. Then a few days before you were due I got word that the Gestapo suddenly had arrived at N—, were quartered right on the Blois estate. I sent a message over, urging that the landing be changed. I never got an answer. I thought the pigeon had been caught. So I waited. There was a chance that I might reach you and get you away. So I planned the sabotage of a bridge nearby to draw their attention away. But it didn't work. When we got to N— the whole place for miles around was guarded. I was afraid they knew about you. I had to make a decision. There was no justification for risking a whole organization if they were after one man. I almost got caught myself. I hung around, you see, for a few more days and sent a man into the village to try to find out. He came back and reported that the Germans had shot the American and that they couldn't understand why I hadn't been caught. It was obviously a case of treason."

He stopped, looking at Chet. Slowly a smile broke in his face. "But here you are," he said.

"Did you ever suspect any particular person?"

"No," answered Grandelieu hesitantly. "Not at the time."

"But lately?" asked Chet.

A silence fell. Then Grandelieu said, "Lately . . . yes . . . it sounds insane in a way. That person is a well-known man, held in high esteem. I never had any reason to mistrust him during all these years. He ran considerable risk himself, was parachuted several times into occupied France, establishing contacts. Then . . ."

Chet saw the face of the guard pop up behind the little window in the door. He went across the cell and very politely, appealing to the man's sense of importance, asked him if it was all right to go on talking. When he came back to the window, Grandelieu spoke hurriedly.

"For a short time we used Josephine Vachon to spy on a German . . . a civilian living in Paris. She got a job there as a maid. The German had many visitors, important ones, among them people we had never suspected of playing a double game. Well, it seems that this same personality, several times when we thought he was in London, was among his guests. At least when he came back after the liberation of France she thought she recognized him from the photos in the papers. She told me. It seemed impossible. Then one day she saw him on the street, very clearly. She came to me that evening and swore it was no mistake."

"What did you do?"

"I tried to find any kind of trace which could prove her accusation. If she was right, then this man never had taken any risks, then the Germans knew when he was coming and knew what he was reporting back to London. Then, too, he must have been the man who betrayed the American at N—. We had almost discovered a link when she died."

"She was murdered," said Chet again. "And when you tried to find out if she died a natural death you were arrested. So Pierre . . ."

Grandelieu looked startled. "It's dangerous for you to know too much."

"I'm used to danger," Chet said. "Listen—"

He told his story quickly. Grandelieu listened intently and when Chet had finished, suddenly lifted both hands to his face and Chet could see his shoulders shaking. After a long while, Grandelieu finally spoke again.

"Millions of people have died, millions have suffered.

Whole generations all over the world have been ruined, women unable to bear children, men not able to . . . children are starving—and men like him just to achieve power or fame . . ." He broke off, then went on: "You believe in the good because you want to believe in it. You fight to spread your faith in it because it seems the only way to spend your life and then in the end . . . the same tensions— strikes, revolutions, civil wars, maybe another war. They are in every country and what can we do. . . ." He looked up at Chet and added bitterly, calmly, "Go home . . . go home at once . . . leave your hands off this affair . . . it's dangerous . . . go home for Sue's sake."

There was silence in which only the steps of the guard outside on the corridor could be heard and the singing of the river below the prison.

Chet said, "You are charged with Intelligence with the enemy but have you any idea what they will present in evidence against you?"

"None," said Grandelieu. "You see I did not find the man I wanted in Rouen. He was dead. But I am reasonably certain that I was arrested here because I was trying to find him. That I was close to the truth. Also it was easier to keep it quiet, here where I am not known. Of course I will be given a lawyer and, though most of these cases drag out, I feel sure that mine will be hurried through. I won't be given a chance to find the witnesses I need to prove my innocence. No, I can't imagine what evidence against me could be presented."

Chet said nothing. Presently he heard Grandelieu's voice again:

"And nobody ever will succeed in proving anything against Pierre. . . . He is careful, cautious. Josephine is dead, so are two other people who possibly knew something. Both died in accidents. I could never find out how. And if someone else tries to fight him he, too, will die. As I will. I will repeat that I am innocent but I will not drag in friends or name witnesses who, if they testify for me, only would be endangered. So . . ." Again he shrugged his shoulders.

"You're foolish, man!" protested Chet.

Grandelieu shook his head. And his gesture was such that Chet knew there was no use trying to persuade the man to give him any names.

"Sue!" said Robert suddenly. "I love her very much. Take my advice. Go back to Paris and take care in getting back, otherwise . . ." and he smiled, "It would be such a waste if both of us . . . Well, get back and arrange to get out of Europe as quickly as possible. They are flying Americans home and I should think you rate a ride. And take Sue with you or make her follow you."

"By the way," said Chet, "Sue trusts you. There has not been one moment when she has wavered. I must confess I . . ."

"I have an old friend in the cotton mills here," Robert said. "Gabriel. Just ask for Gabriel. He'll get you transportation. It's important that you get back to Paris quickly. To hang around here is dangerous, even . . ." and he smiled at Chet's clothes.

Then the smile died in his eyes, his face clouded and suddenly he looked very tired.

"We can't escape our fate, can we?" he said. "I am

glad you came. I am glad you are alive. Tell Sue not to worry too much. There is always one beautiful thing left, the knowledge that life goes on, regardless of what we make of it. It goes on and on, renewing itself. One can always hope that it will be a little better every time."

He held out his hand and clasped Chet's for a minute, then he turned away, standing as he had stood when Chet had entered, a tall, rigid, lonely figure leaning against bars.

For a little while Chet did not move, trying to find words, then finally he crossed the cell and knocked at the door, calling gently for the guard.

The man came, opened and relocked the door, led Chet back through the corridors, into the warden's office where he signed a made-up name in an indecipherable scrawl on the slip which acknowledged that he had been admitted and talked to the prisoner Grandelieu. The guard then took him out, passed him on to another man who led him across the courtyard and out to the big gate, which opened and closed behind him with a loud shriek of its unoiled hinges.

He looked back once, up to the row of barred windows, but he could not see Robert Grandelieu.

Chet went straight across the bridge and on to the small island in the Seine where the cotton mills were. He was directed to Gabriel, who sat on a staircase, warming himself in the sunshine of the morning. To his surprise Gabriel was a boy of hardly sixteen. When he heard the doctor's name his eyes lit up.

"Give him my best when you get to Paris," he said.

He had no idea that his friend was in the prison a few stone-throws away.

"He told me it very much depended on you if and when I get back to Paris," Chet said and saw the boy bite his lip with pride.

"There are trains going to Paris now," he said, "and if one knows the engineer and is not afraid, one can ride with him in his cabin."

"Well, do you, Gabriel?" asked Chet.

"It's settled," the boy told him.

Chet reached Paris about two o'clock. Outside the station the big square was black with people, most of them women, waiting, waiting days and nights, hour after hour, in rain and sunshine, for the trains which were still carrying back Frenchmen from Germany, prisoners, slave laborers. No one knew for certain when they would arrive.

He needed almost an hour to get to the hotel where Susan lived. When he came into the lobby he could see her through the wide-open glass door, sitting outside in the little garden under a pink and forget-me-not-blue striped umbrella. She was alone. Chet went out and across the flagstones, smelling the hydrangeas in their big green pots, which had been placed around and below the stone wall to make it appear more a garden than the little backyard it really was.

"Sue," he said softly, "don't say anything right now . . . go upstairs and in a little while I will follow you. Just pretend I'm a priest collecting money."

Sue, her eyes politely indifferent, reached for her purse and pulled out a small bill.

"I think I have been watched," she murmured. She stood up from her chair and nodded. "But if I have, I lost him finally in the Louvre." Smilingly she moved away. Chet could hear the heels of her shoes making a soft clicking noise on the flagstones. After a while he followed her inside the hotel and went quickly upstairs, avoiding the lift as he had the very first time when he didn't want the heavenly moment to pass too rapidly after four long years.

Her door stood ajar and he entered quickly, closing it gently and locking it after him. Again across the street, leaning in the frame of the open window, was the boy with his violin. Sue, following the direction of his glance, without having to be told, moved across the room to shut the French window to the small balcony and lowered the shade. Then she turned, her breath coming unevenly.

"Chet," she said, "what does all this mean? Where have you been? I was frantic when we were disconnected. Why didn't you try me again? I didn't dare to leave the room. I thought any moment you would phone. Where have you been?"

Chet went into her bathroom without answering, turned the water on, reached for a glass and drank thirstily, hastily, then bent and slapped the cold water against his face. All the way back to Paris he had racked his brain to discover a way out, to think of some way to help Robert; but only now, standing there in the sedate, white windowless bathroom, did he admit to himself that he was helpless for the moment.

There was, he knew, nothing he could do. Now, even though he was certain of Grandelieu's innocence and sure that the man he was after was Pierre Blois, he could not move. Chester Burton still had to remain dead and Paul Mercier was drowned in the Seine.

If he should go to his colonel submitting all of the data he had gathered, it still would not be enough. The final proof was still missing. Nor could he call in the help of the French police. They might inadvertently warn Blois of the charges that had been brought against him. He'd simply have to go on searching, but what about Grandelieu?

"Tell me," said Sue from the door, "tell me quickly what happened. You got the pass. So Blois was kind. Did you see Robert?"

He came back into her room, the white rough bathrobe which the hotel still furnished wrapped around him. He sat down on the bed, then gradually stretched out on it.

"Did you see Robert?" he heard Sue asking again. The anxiety in her voice. He lifted his head and stared at her. She was very pale and the few freckles across the small proud bridge of her nose stood out as if they were pasted onto it.

If he wanted to help Robert then he had no other choice but to postpone his own search, to drop it for the time being, at least until Grandelieu could be freed.

Grandelieu and Sue.

Chet sighed.

The decision was not easy for him. For too many years had he longed for the moment when he would have covered the first half of this job, when he would know who the man was . . . Grandelieu or Blois . . .

and could embark on the second half . . . to find the proof.

He felt the inside of his mouth go dry again.

"No," he said. "No, Sue. I didn't see Robert."

He watched her take one step in his direction, the reproach in her eyes, the dawn of desperation in her face. He said quickly, "Something happened, darling, don't be upset. I decided I didn't need to see Robert to believe you."

She was right, he thought fleetingly. He is decent, honest. By the way Sue sat down in a chair he could tell her relief. From far away he imagined he could hear Grandelieu's voice, "I love her very much . . . go home . . . go back to America . . . take Sue with you . . . for Sue's sake."

"I will do anything in my power to help him," he said.

"I knew you would. Once you were certain that he is innocent, I knew you would." Her voice was small with happiness.

"It won't be easy," he reminded her.

Again he looked at her and the faint idea forming in his mind seemed to carry too much risk, seemed too dangerous for Sue. And he knew that he personally could not take part in anything if Blois was to feel safe. He sighed again. He said:

"Sue, I want you to remember that Paul Mercier does not exist any longer. You last saw him two days ago."

Her eyes were on him, widening, but she did not ask any questions. He was grateful for that.

"As Chester Burton is officially dead and Paul

Mercier no longer exists, it's all up to you, Sue."

There was a slight pause, then Sue said, "What does that mean?" It means a trap, thought Chet, a trap for Pierre Blois, the only trap I can think of right now that might work. But he couldn't tell her that. To carry through his plan he needed an absolutely trusting Sue, a Sue who would not have suspicions of her own, an uncomplicated Sue.

"You love Robert, don't you?"

"If you are asking me if I am willing to do anything possible in my power . . . I would do anything, Chet, anything for him."

"Of course I do, Robert," he thought, "of course I do, Robert. I would do anything for him." Again he saw the rigid lonely figure of Grandelieu in the prison cell. It's just another joke of life, he thought. One of those silly situations one reads or hears about and which seem so incredible until they happen to one personally. He pulled himself together.

"I have found out a great deal about Grandelieu," he said, "but it was impossible to find out what the evidence is they hold against him."

"Yes?" she said.

"Sue," he asked, "will you take the chance of being expelled? It's important that the news of Grandelieu's arrest be made public. And the charge that is made. Do you have enough friends who will take your word for it and print the story?"

"Yes," said Sue; and after a slight pause, "How much do you want them to print?"

Chet turned his head towards the window and watched the sun make designs on the shade, flickering waves of light. There had been hours when he had thought that he would never see the sun again as a free man.

It was essential, he was certain, to put Pierre Blois in a spot, to tie him up with Grandelieu somehow. Someone would have to make a statement. Blois and Grandelieu had worked together. What would be more natural than a reporter asking Blois for an interview?

"Oh, just the facts," he said. "Dr. Robert Grandelieu arrested, charged with Intelligence with the enemy. The same Robert Grandelieu who played such an important part during the early days of the German occupation, when he worked in the underground in connection with Pierre Blois in London."

"I didn't know that," said Sue.

"It's true," Chet told her. "What will Pierre Blois say? Will he come out for Grandelieu or against him? Colonel Blois, one of the few men who knew him so well. Paris is looking forward to his attitude. Something like that . . ."

6

Pierre Blois did not say anything.

The papers had come out carrying headlines about Grandelieu's arrest. Making the most of it, spreading it in their columns. Commentators got on the air. Public opinion stirred. Journalists were storming the colonel's office and surrounding his private house. But there was a guard around the colonel and nobody could get through.

Anyhow, thought Chet, now they can't kill Grandelieu off. He has to be alive for the trial.

Then on the second day after the news had been published, Pierre Blois's secretary handed out a release. The careful statement of a cautious man. Colonel Blois was sorry not to be able to make any comment. But on such a charge everyone, including himself, would have to wait for the trial, when undoubtedly the truth would emerge.

Chet was still staying in Sue's room. An unregistered visitor at the Atala. And Sue was staying out at night, sleeping in the apartment of a friend, while her room was being redecorated.

"I swear I am being shadowed," she said on the afternoon when the noncommittal release came out. She tossed several editions of newspapers angrily to the floor. "Who in the world could be interested in spying on every one of my moves?"

Blois, of course, thought Chet. The introduction for Paul Mercier had originally come through Susan Porter. Undoubtedly he had learned that much.

Aloud he said:

"Well, after all, you and Grandelieu were seen together. It seems quite logical."

She turned on him. "You still seem to doubt Robert. Yes, you do," she added before he could interrupt her. "You promised to help. And what are you doing? Nothing. Just hiding in my room. God knows why!"

"Sue," he said very quietly, "you must trust me. You have to trust me. I've got a plan . . . maybe it will be successful . . . in the meantime . . ."

"In the meantime," she said hotly, nervously, "I

cannot help thinking of Robert behind bars, cannot help thinking that by the attitude Pierre Blois takes, he also takes the fire out of the whole affair. People will settle down and imitate his attitude." She shrugged her shoulders and spread her hands. "The trial will prove it . . . let's wait till the trial . . . even Blois who knew him so well waits for the trial . . . why stick our necks out if he doesn't? This scoop was your idea, Chet . . . I don't know what you were hoping for . . ."

Chet lighted a cigarette, slowly, carefully, concentrating on his match as if its little flame and the time it burned were of utmost importance. He was thinking rapidly.

"Sue," he said calmly. "You've met Blois. Why don't you personally appeal to him on Grandelieu's behalf?"

He was certain that Blois was behind Grandelieu's arrest. If Blois could only be trapped into revealing what evidence was against Grandelieu . . .

"Yes," he said again, "why don't you go and see Blois, Sue? Didn't you tell me he plays up to Americans?"

He was thinking intently and clearly. It might be a chance. The only chance left for Robert. And if she was being shadowed at Blois's order it would be better to send her right into the lion's den and thereby destroy any suspicion Blois might have about her and her connections with Grandelieu.

"I don't know why I didn't think of that myself," said Sue.

Chet shrugged his shoulders. "Neither of us did, apparently," he said. "But it appears as if Blois might be the only real source of help. Go and ask him. Just .

. ." he hesitated. "Sue," he said, "just tell him that you like Grandelieu, have known him for a long time. You were so upset when you heard of his arrest from his friend. Remember, it was Paul Mercier who told you about Grandelieu's arrest. It was Paul Mercier who asked you to intervene and get him an introduction to some important man . . . and it was your friend the Comte de Roland who suggested Blois."

"Yes," she said slowly, looking squarely at him, her eyes unwavering; and for a moment he wondered how he could let her take such a risk. "And if he should ask me if I have seen Paul Mercier lately?"

"You haven't," he said. "Not since you got him the introduction. After all, Mercier did not mean anything to you. You bothered only because he is a friend of Grandelieu. You don't even know if he got the pass he wanted."

Had Grandelieu ever told her of his suspicions about Blois? Had Grandelieu ever mentioned to Sue what the Vachon had told him? No, he decided. He was too careful a man, too cautious a man. And he remembered vividly the first minutes he had spent in Grandelieu's cell at Rouen. He had denied knowing Sue, because he knew how dangerous it might be to have her involved.

Sue came over to where Chet sat and perched on the arm of his chair. She rested her hand lightly on his head. But he didn't see her eyes just then, he only felt her fingers. He wanted to hold her then, to tell her everything, to warn her, try to tell her how to behave, but he knew he couldn't do it. The more innocent she was the better chance Robert stood, and

Sue, too, for that matter.

"I will try to get to him," she said. "I think I understand."

"Remember," he told her, "it's the evidence you want. Try to find out what they are holding against him. Nothing else matters. And remember that you haven't seen Paul Mercier for days. And that you're not concerned about Mercier. And Sue . . . try to remember every word he says. Each little word might be important, might give us a clue, a chance to help Robert . . ."

"You don't need to remind me of that," said Sue.

He didn't know how long he had been asleep when he was awakened by the crash of thunder. That's why I was so tired suddenly, he thought, turning round, content to have found an explanation for the sleepiness which so often at unexpected moments overcame him. He remembered how Sue had teased him during childhood days. "There'll be a storm," she would say. "Chet is yawning."

Again he turned and now rested on his back, his arms crossed under his head, watching the storm through the window. The lightning flashed, long streaks of electricity zigzagging across the sky, lighting the low-hanging clouds, and again the crash as if a bomb had found its target.

Suddenly he grew aware that Sue wasn't there, Sue who was scared of thunderstorms, who back in Elmira when the storms were heavy and the current would fail, leaving the house dark and the refrigerator without its murmur, would run up to hide in her bed, hauling the sheets over her head, torn between the Sunday school lesson teaching it was God's voice speaking beyond the clouds, and her father's realistic cursing, "Bedamn, I haven't had a childbirth in years that didn't occur in a storm." She concluded finally that maybe it was the same, God's words manifesting themselves in a new life.

No. Sue wasn't there. It was past four o'clock, and she had promised to come in at the latest at two.

He sat up, wide awake suddenly though the air was still heavy and the rain hadn't brought any relief. Where could Sue be?

Blois, he thought. "Blois," the lightning seemed to spell, flashing through the sky; "Blois," the thunder crashed; "Blois," the rain sang as it fell in fast heavy drops. Blois. Maybe she got the appointment with Blois. And she couldn't phone and tell me because I told her not to, not to make herself conspicuous.

Blois.

He should never have advised her to go. It was all his fault. Because he couldn't go himself he had sent her.

"I must have been insane," he said aloud. Blois must be suspicious of her. But what could he do? She is an American. He wouldn't dare do anything. Not that way. At the most he could have her expelled from the country. But could he be sure? Hadn't Grandelieu said "accidents"? How about himself and the river?

And if Blois had trapped her? If Blois had trapped Sue instead of Sue trapping him? He was smart, he knew the world, people, women. What if he found out from Sue what he must not find out . . . that Chester

Burton was alive . . . that Chester Burton and Mercier were identical?

But no, he told himself. Sue is intelligent. Don't underrate Sue. He thought frantically of moments which showed clearly that Sue possessed unusual intelligence, intuition and discretion. He remembered too, the quiet way with which she had listened to his stories, never questioning, never betraying how much she believed of them.

He heard a key turning in the lock. He swung around. For a moment he was flooded with relief on seeing her standing there, alive, unharmed.

"Hello," he said.

"Hello," said Sue. She turned and locked the door again, then came into the room, took off her gloves and sat down in the chair near the window.

"It's sticky in here, isn't it?"

She lowered the shade and opened the French windows. The shade began to flap against the frame of the balcony door. The thunder sounded louder, nearer.

"Chet," she said, "it's a hopeless mess."

She leaned back into her chair and reached for a package of cigarettes on the little table next to it. "Why didn't you tell me where you were going?" he said as he watched her strike the match on the sole of her shoe, holding it up and finally bringing the flame to meet the cigarette.

"I didn't know myself," she answered slowly. "You see I was having lunch at Maxim's. I went there for an interview and suddenly I saw Blois come in. He was alone. I watched him. And then I thought this was as good an opportunity as any other so I just walked over and introduced myself."

"Yes," said Chet, "yes?" He could almost see Sue leaving her table, crossing the small dining room and stopping before Blois.

"He was very courteous," Sue went on. "He said he remembered my note, but he hadn't found time to answer it and give me an hour when he would be free. He was almost through with lunch and when he got up I just followed him out. I was not going to be shaken off."

"What did you say? Can you remember precisely what you said and the answers he made?"

"Yes," said Sue. "When we came out to the street I told him that I hadn't wanted to see him for an interview. That it was quite true that I meant to do a profile on him for my magazine but that I had written him because I wanted him to help me. 'I'd be delighted to help you, mademoiselle,' he said, 'but you don't look like anyone who needs help,' and he looked at me for a long time, smilingly."

Chet remembered Blois's smile—the artificial generous smile he had had for Mercier. He could visualize Blois now, standing there next to Sue, taking her in, all of her, as he flattered her smoothly.

"But I do," I said, "because Robert Grandelieu is a very good friend of mine. 'Grandelieu,' he said. And then there was a pause. I tried to read something in his face but there was nothing. We walked on in silence."

She took another drag at her cigarette. "And then he said, 'Does he mean a lot to you, mademoiselle?' I didn't know what to answer. So I was silent and he, too, said nothing; and I thought maybe it was best to let him think whatever he wanted to."

Chet nodded. A hundred questions formed in his mind, but he did not want to disturb or distract her.

"We walked a few blocks and finally I said, 'Colonel Blois, I believe that Robert Grandelieu is innocent. I know him so well. You see, that was why I asked the Comte de Roland to make it possible for one of Robert's friends to see you, Paul Mercier.'"

Chet shifted.

"'Mercier,' Blois said. 'Mercier,' as if he couldn't remember right offhand. 'Paul Mercier. Yes, I remember now. So that's why Roland was so urgent.' He smiled again, then added, 'What kind of a man is Mercier?'"

Sue got up from her chair and began to pace the room. "I said that I couldn't tell because I knew him only slightly. But that it was through him that I had first heard of Grandelieu's arrest, and that then, of course, I was vitally interested."

For a second Chet could not remember if he had told Sue to say that it had been through Mercier that she knew about the affair or if she had said it on her own impulse.

"You know, Chet," said Sue, "I don't like Blois. I have heard a lot about him and read a lot about him. I thought I would like him but I didn't . . ."

"Never mind," he interrupted her shortly, "go on."

"He asked me if I knew he had given him a pass, but I said I hadn't heard from him since and that probably Mercier was trying to get to Rouen. Then I took the plunge. I said I knew that he, Blois, had worked with Grandelieu and must have found him trustworthy and a patriot ready to do anything for his country and that he simply must make a statement to that effect because so many of the people Robert had worked with were either dead by now or had gone back to America so that there would be no time to gather enough witnesses. He was silent again and we were walking fast. Then finally he said, 'Mademoiselle, you must understand my position. I can do nothing before the trial. Nothing, mademoiselle. Nothing.'"

A sudden gust of wind suddenly swept a spray of raindrops into the room and for a second the shade, like a kite, was carried up and out onto the balcony.

"So I bluffed," said Sue. "I told him that then I would get in touch through the Embassy and my paper with people who had known Robert in the early days and through whom I originally met Robert."

"What did he say then?"

"He took a long time and then he said, 'I wouldn't do that, mademoiselle, if I were you.' 'Why not?' I asked him. 'If you cannot help him because of your position . . . somebody must help him.' 'Mademoiselle,' he said, 'do you think I seem to be a man who wouldn't risk public opinion to help an innocent man? Do you think I wouldn't do anything in the world to aid a comrade whom I have found trustworthy? Do you think I would keep quiet and avoid any statement if I had not good reason?'"

"Yes?" said Chet. He could imagine Blois rolling out those words, those beautiful, big, proud words. He could imagine Blois's face and the sincerity and anguish in his cold arrogant eyes.

"I was horrified," said Sue. "I hadn't expected that. Not that. Had you, Chet?"

"No," he answered.

"I was so startled," repeated Sue, "that he noticed it. He put his hand on my arm. 'I am sorry, mademoiselle,' he said. 'I am most sincerely sorry. I did not believe it myself. I was just as shocked as you are now; but there is no doubt, no doubt at all, that Grandelieu played a double game.' 'Never,' I told him. 'Never.' I said we had to find people to prove it couldn't be true. Blois shook his head, he said . . .'"

"Go on!"

Sue suddenly put her face between her hands. "There is a report about a note brought back by someone who had been imprisoned for years by the Germans until just recently . . . It was written by a man who said that he had been betrayed by Grandelieu."

"Say that again," ordered Chet.

Sue repeated her last words.

"What else did he say?"

"That, of course, he had my word of honor not to mention this . . . for he knew it only because when he had first heard about Grandelieu's arrest he had immediately gone to the police to tell them that he, Colonel Blois, would personally vouch for Robert. So they had shown him the note, and asked him if he were still willing to vouch for Robert." Sue's voice trembled.

Chet looked up into her eyes. He saw the despair spreading over Sue's face. But he couldn't tell if she was confused, torn between her own sure instinct and the undeniable fact of a note which proved Grandelieu a traitor. The frown on her forehead deepened and for a second Chet thought that she would break down and cry. Instead she went on, her voice very small.

"I told Blois that I couldn't believe it. That it all must be a mistake. A horrible mistake. But Blois shook his head. He said he had thought that, too . . . but the note which accused Grandelieu was written by an American whom Blois had known personally."

"By an American?"

Chet saw her nod, saw her lips moving, but no longer could he hear what she was saying.

By an American, he thought. By an American whom Blois knew personally? At the particular time when he had been dropped into occupied France to establish contacts there with the maquis, there had been few Americans sent to France. Later, yes . . . but he had been one of the very first . . . and of those who *had* gone not many had been caught by the Germans.

His mind was spinning, one thought chasing the other. He leaned back, fixing his glance on the ceiling, on a spot where the plaster was slightly cracked and had not been repaired yet. It couldn't be, he thought . . . and yet it was only logical. Wouldn't it be ironical if he, Chet, trying to save Robert, should find the proof he had to have?

"Chet," said Sue, but he didn't answer. And why shouldn't it be? he thought. Blois knows that Chester Burton was caught, shot by the Germans right there on his estate. A dead man can't be a witness. A dead man's signature to a letter which turns up miraculously after many years . . .

He began with an effort to sort out his thoughts. The Vachon had been murdered because she had recognized Blois as the same man who had had dealings with the Germans at a time when he was not supposed to be in France. And Blois, aware of her friendship with Grandelieu, had watched every move of the latter. At the same time a released prisoner of war, Paul Mercier, turns up in N— to question the villagers there about an American. Had questioned the Mole on the Blois estate. The Mole, who was an employee of Blois, undoubtedly had notified the colonel. From then on Paul Mercier had been watched . . . had been seen visiting Grandelieu's office, going to the only man in France who, outside of Blois, knew about Chester Burton. Grandelieu, in turn, had set out for Rouen. And Blois, afraid that Grandelieu was getting close to the truth and that the whole affair might suddenly be exposed . . . had acted. So that he could never be accused of Intelligence with the enemy he had chosen what he must have considered safe evidence—evidence of a dead man—and charged Robert with his own crime. And Paul Mercier as a possible threat had been drowned.

"I went to find the evidence against Robert, but . . ." said Sue.

The note written by an American! Who had written it, who had submitted it to the police? Blois! There was no longer any doubt in Chet's mind.

"It all must be a horrible mistake," Sue said again.

No, thought Chet. This is no mistake. This all has been well planned. The same old forces working again, the same forces which have always led to war. And, as always, they are using the same methods: murder, lies and the defamation of those who try to fight them, accusing their opponents of the very crimes they were committing.

And I, he wondered, what can I do? If I am wrong, if Blois is not using the dead Chester Burton, then how can I help Robert? And if I am right and turn up alive, Blois will say that he acted in good faith or find a patsy to take the rap. But, in any case, Blois will get out scot-free . . . just as powerful, allowed to go on with his dirty work. And I have no proof against him. I cannot even prove that he tried to murder Paul Mercier . . . a most regrettable accident but surely no one could hold Blois responsible. The chauffeur certainly would never reappear.

"What are you thinking, Chet?"

Chet got up and went over to where Sue sat in her chair. He put one hand on her shoulder. He could feel through the thin cotton of her dress the effort she was making to hold herself erect.

"Of home," he said. "And how much I would like to be there right now, sailing up the Hudson . . ."

Sue slumped a little. "Oh, Chet," she said, "we must not give up. We must find a way to help Robert. You *can't* give up."

"Don't worry," he told her. "You asked me what I was thinking . . . No, I haven't given up . . . not yet."

The note written by an American! He must find out if it was signed, as he suspected, with his name. That was the next step. Forget everything else. One thing at a time . . . and then, perhaps, there would be a chance. A chance to prove to Blois that his game was up. To corner Blois. How? How in the world could he ever find out?

Suddenly he thought he saw a way. Blois felt safe. If Blois could be caught off guard, startled into . . . It was the most dangerous way but the only possibility. I must go myself, Chet decided.

He moved away from Sue, sat down in front of the small writing desk. He took one sheet out of the folder and then another one. Quickly writing, he put down the story of Chester Burton, Mercier and as much as he knew of Robert Grandelieu.

"What are you going to do?" asked Sue. He turned, folding the sheets of paper and sealing the envelope. He smiled at her. For a second the temptation to take her into his arms rose in him. She looked pale and tired but he thought he had never before seen her so beautiful.

"I don't want to tell you," he said gently. "Just trust me, Sue. And if, by any chance, you shouldn't hear from me . . . if you don't hear from me by tomorrow morning at ten, take this letter at once to my colonel." He went quickly towards the door.

"Chet," she said. "Chet, you must . . ."

Chet pulled the door shut after him.

When Chet turned into the small, quiet side street he saw that tonight it was alive with vehicles. Several army and staff cars stood parked along the curb; a few high old taxis and horse-drawn cabs were driving up and away, their drivers cursing for their own amusement as they tried to reverse in the narrow space.

The front door of Pierre Blois's house stood open, guarded by a tall, dignified servant who, in his white knee breeches, silk stockings and black pumps, seemed to have materialized from another world for the sole purpose of demonstrating that the glamorous, ostentatious times to which his costume belonged would return, too, someday . . . at least, if Pierre Blois had his way.

He glanced arrogantly at Chet's uniform, borrowed an hour before from his colonel when he had told him his quest was nearly at an end. With a gesture of his white-gloved hand, he motioned to other servants. One of them held open the second door leading into the hall of the house.

"This way, monsieur."

There were American officers' caps lying or hanging on the hatrack. Chet put his among them. So what people were saying was true—Pierre Blois was carefully nursing relations with the Allies. His colonel had said as much when he told Chet of the party. In the large mirror he caught a glimpse of the big salon. It was crowded. Evening dresses and uniforms with a few civilian white ties. Feathers and flowers in the high coiffures of women. Here and there, like a bird opening its wings, a fan, once again in style, would unfold. Above the heads of the crowd, laden trays on upstretched arms, swinging slightly on strained muscles, were expertly balanced by the hired waiters.

Chet came out of the anteroom looking at the palms of his hands intently and critically.

"Where could I wash up a little?" he asked a footman

coming out of the salon. The tray the man carried was almost empty except for two untouched glasses of champagne. Chet reached for one, drank slowly, thinking how ridiculous it was that he should have his first glass of champagne in the house of the man who had betrayed him.

"To your left, sir. Third door to the left."

Chet put the empty glass back, nodded and walked quickly along the corridor. He opened the second door and found what he had hoped for, and had seen the last time he was in the house, the back staircase. He turned, pretending to have made a mistake. The footman had vanished through another door into the kitchen or pantry. There was no one visible right then. He gently pulled the door shut behind him. There was no carpet on the back staircase and he moved cautiously on tiptoe.

After twelve steps there was another door. Behind it he heard the laughter of women. He stood still, leaning against the door, then gradually bent and brought his eyes to a crack in the frame. This door led into the upstairs hall. He could see flashes of light, elegant colors rushing by. Then suddenly steps in his direction. He pulled back, flattening himself against the wall. Very clearly he could hear a high voice calling:

"Where are you going, Belle? We go down here."

And another, much younger voice answered, "I can never resist getting lost in a house. It's such fun to find out how people live when they don't know you are looking."

The first voice reproached. *"Enfant terrible!* Come over here quickly!"

Everything grew quiet. After a long while Chet pressed the handle gently down. The upstairs hall was empty. Opposite from where he stood the door to a room hung open. Evening wraps and coats were lying on a couch, on several chairs and across a bed. He went straight into it. Should someone find him there he would say simply that a lady had left her handbag upstairs.

There were two doors. He opened the one in the left wall and came into a bathroom. From it a small white painted door led into what he realized at once must be Pierre Blois's dressing room. It was a narrow towel-shaped room with only one window looking out onto the street. Two large wardrobes, a divan upholstered in purple plush, a dressing table and a safe. An open door led into the bedroom.

The bedroom was surprisingly large with three windows overlooking the garden. Across two of them the curtains were already drawn. In front of the third, which was open, stood an armchair and a standing lamp. Except for these two pieces it was Spartanly furnished. The bed was narrow, almost an army cot. Its covers had already been opened for the night. Chet nodded to himself, satisfied. No servant, then, would bother him. Next to it was a table with a radio, a telephone, a lamp and a tray with a water carafe and a glass. That was all. The walls were bare, no pictures, paintings, no mirrors, no decoration except for two large photographs which showed the factories Pierre Blois owned.

Chet sat down in the chair.

Slowly time dragged on, interrupted once in a while

when doors downstairs opened and closed, by voices, laughter and later by music. As the night grew darker some of the guests began to stream into the garden below his window. Scraps of conversation were carried up to him on a light tender night breeze. Then the moon began to rise, its light gaining strength and throwing a silver stream into the window and across the floor.

From the silver stream Sue seemed to lift herself on her elbows, turning her head slightly in his direction.

"What a beautiful night," she said. "Look at the moon, Chet. Such a lovely moon. And how the grass smells. We must never forget this night, Chet. Whatever may happen, we must never forget this night and our meadow with the moon shining."

She sank back into the dewy, sweetly scented grass and the moonlight began to flicker. It flickered over London and someone, he had forgotten who, said: "It's a bomber's moon. Tonight they'll come. It's a Hitler moon all right."

Then it stopped flickering, was falling into an airless, crowded barrack, and an old man sharing Chet's small space poked him in the ribs. "Hey you, you better watch out for Auguste. He always walks in the full moon and the swine will only be too glad to pretend he's trying to escape and shoot him." And he could see the boy Auguste, pale and haggard, struggling.

Now, in this moonlight, Chet thought about Robert and Sue. Robert who, like himself, had been betrayed by Blois. Sue, whom they both loved. Without Robert he probably would not be sitting here in the colonel's room. And, without Chet, Robert would probably not have the slightest chance.

It was always the same, for everyone, the decision between the two things—love and duty. The satisfaction of one's own desires or a clean conscience. The old temptation to resign oneself. "I can't change the world, the world will go on, people will go on the way they always have . . ." but, like Robert, he had learned to believe that that wasn't quite true. At least, that wasn't all.

From outside came the sound of motors being started, cars rolling away, the trot of horses on cement, the slamming of doors, laughter, whistles, the clicking of heels. The last bar played on a piano, the last clatter of dishes.

And time went on and the moon rose and Chet was waiting. The house grew quiet, began to breathe, to whisper. Now, now, now.

Steps coming up the staircase, the opening of the door to the dressing room. The closing of the same door. Steps, closer now. Halting. A deep yawn, a slight thudding noise which told Chet that Blois had sat down on the divan. The rustle of papers being turned over. Blois apparently was reading a late newspaper. Then steps again moving in the direction of the bathroom. Water spurting into the tub. And again steps, the slight noise of a door handle being turned carelessly. Pierre Blois entered his bedroom. He came in yawning, loosening the belt around his tunic, opening the collar around his throat, moving through the dark room towards his bed, stretching out his hand to pull the cord of the lamp.

"Good evening, Colonel Blois," said Chet. He didn't

move. He sat in the chair near the open window, straight, motionless.

Just for a second the bewilderment so clearly visible on Blois's face portrayed his thoughts. First, recognition of a man whom he had thought dead; then the astonishment with which he stared at the American uniform; then, surprisingly quickly, the determination not to be bluffed.

"Who are you?" Blois asked coldly.

Chet rose. His movements were slow, casual. Well, here it is, he thought.

7

"I must apologize, colonel," he said. "I am sorry for this rather informal visit, but I wanted to avoid any kind of attention. I am sure you will understand my reasons, colonel. I am not Paul Mercier. I am an American Intelligence officer investigating the peculiar circumstances which led to the death of one of our men. You were very helpful to a man called Paul Mercier who asked you to make it possible for him to see Grandelieu. I must again express my gratitude." He paused, looking at Blois innocently.

"Unfortunately," he added, "we had bad luck. Shortly before we reached Rouen the chauffeur lost control of the car and we plunged into the Seine."

"*Mon Dieu,*" said Blois. "No one could explain what had happened when the car didn't get to Rouen. The police are still investigating . . ." He stopped. "I am so happy to see you alive and unharmed. Into the river, you said? Incredible. The chauffeur?"

Chet shrugged.

"I am terribly sorry, terribly sorry . . ."

No one who didn't suspect Blois would believe that he was extending a graceful apology for a murder that had not been successful, an apology to the man who should be dead.

What a rat he is, thought Chet, but a perfect actor, and I . . . I can't even tell him that I'm on to him . . . I am here to help Robert. I've got to find out who the American was who wrote that note . . .

"You must be an excellent swimmer," he heard Blois say. And then quickly, "May I offer you a drink?" Blois stepped backward towards the wall, his hand outstretched to reach the small black button of a bell.

"Don't ring," said Chet. "Please, colonel, remember that I don't want to be seen by anyone. And, thank you, but I don't drink."

Blois withdrew his hand. He watched Blois sit down, then for a minute both were silent. Silent because each of them knew that one incautious word meant danger. Finally Blois snapped his cigarette case open and offered it to Chet.

"No, thank you, colonel . . . I don't smoke either."

"No drink, no cigarettes, what then can I do for you?" Blois was smoking now, sitting on the end of his bed, blowing small, perfect rings of smoke into the air.

Chet kept his conversational casual tone.

"I came to ask if, by any chance, you remember a man named Chester Burton?"

He paused again. Blois didn't answer. He continued to blow little rings. Chet was forced to speak on.

"We think," he said, "or rather we have reason to believe, that Burton's landing in France was betrayed to the Germans." Again he paused, hoping Blois would speak. But Blois didn't change his attitude of a polite listener.

"In the course of my investigations," continued Chet, "our suspicion turned out to be correct." He stopped for a second. The little rings of smoke still floated from Blois's lips. "Therefore," Chet said, "it seemed wiser to meet Grandelieu not as an officer but as a Frenchman."

"I understand," said Blois. He lighted a new cigarette on the stub of the first one. Then he looked squarely at Chet. No, thought Chet, I must not underestimate this man. If I thought that he would ask questions, I made a mistake. He stared back at Blois steadily. "But you see," he said, smiling wryly, "before I could really establish a connection with Grandelieu he was arrested. So I came to you." He decided not to mention yet that he had talked to Robert. "And when I got back after the accident, I heard about a report regarding a note known to you which is in the hands of the police."

Blois crushed his cigarette. "And now you have come to ask for further information." He nodded comprehendingly.

Chet had not expected this soft willing attitude. If . . . he thought again rapidly . . . if I were in Blois's place, how would I act? If I, as the criminal, found myself opposite an American Intelligence officer, wouldn't I . . . ?

"I would be very grateful indeed," he said, bowing

slightly, "if you would help with my investigation."

Blois stood up, crossing his arms over his chest, and began to pace the room. His face was grave and, when he finally spoke, his voice sounded embarrassed. "Undoubtedly," he said, "you will understand how difficult it is to furnish information about a compatriot. Particularly about a man whom I have trusted for many years. On the other hand, I know that I cannot refuse your request. I feel I must help our Allies whom we French have to thank for so much."

He swallowed. His face was working. Yes, thought Chet, leaning back in his chair, of course . . . Blois couldn't act in any other way.

"It is," said Blois, his voice low, solemn, "very painful to have to admit that a Frenchman betrayed an American. Unfortunately your suspicions are correct. Grandelieu betrayed an American, a man named Chester Burton . . . that's why he was arrested."

He sat down again, staring in front of him at the floor.

"Of course," said Chet, "Grandelieu denies everything."

"So you saw him?"

Chet nodded. "I saw him. I questioned him. He denies everything."

"I wish," said Blois, "that I could believe him. But, unfortunately, I can't. I have seen a letter . . . a note in which Burton writes that Grandelieu personally delivered him to the Germans."

"But," asked Chet, "couldn't this note be a forgery . . . by someone who for personal reasons wants to avenge himself on Grandelieu?"

His left hand in his pocket touched the packet of cigarettes and he had to remind himself sharply that he had pretended not to smoke.

"No," said Blois. "I thought that, too, for a moment. Wanted to think it. But the letter was signed by a code name. Only three persons, Burton, Grandelieu and I, knew this name."

"What was the name?"

"Sagitta," answered Blois.

Sagitta, the room seemed to echo. *Sagitta*. There was the proof Chet had been looking for. The evidence he had needed. And there he sat, he who, by trying to help Robert, had stumbled onto the proof he needed for his own purpose. Sagitta . . . "This note . . ." he said, his voice cold, artificial, "you say you saw it yourself, colonel?"

"Otherwise," said Blois, "I would not dare to make such an accusation."

"One more question," said Chet. "Why, colonel, do you think Grandelieu betrayed Burton?"

Blois took his time. He began hesitantly. "It couldn't have been money," he said. "Grandelieu is rich. Perhaps he himself was threatened and preferred to save his own skin rather than that of an American . . . perhaps he believed in the Nazi ideology . . . who can tell? The trial ought to bring it all out."

"And yet," Chet said carefully, choosing each word, each step, "Grandelieu is known as a fighter for justice. The people love him . . ."

"And that," answered Blois and sighed, "makes him twice as dangerous."

Yes, thought Chet, dangerous to you.

As if he just were being very polite, he rose. "And still," he said, "you, colonel, are just as popular with the people."

Blois smiled politely. "But not quite so dangerous."

"I wonder," said Chet. "I wonder."

"What do you mean?" demanded Blois. He stepped back. "How dare you!"

"Look," said Chet. "Grandelieu will not face a firing squad. It will be you. I am surprised, Pierre Blois, that you don't recognize me. I know I have changed since you wished me *bonne chance* in London after you had already betrayed me to the Germans."

"Chester Burton . . ." murmured Blois, and for the first time appeared shaken. "Chester Burton . . . It is impossible."

"Almost impossible, indeed," said Chet. "You are right, Blois. A man whom you tried to murder twice had little chance really."

Suddenly Blois made a desperate move to steady himself. "You are crazy," he said. "Why should I have murdered you, wanted to murder you? Fantastic! You know my record. I, myself, was parachuted eleven times . . ."

"And came back because it was safe, because the Germans knew you were coming to bring them important information?"

"You have no proof."

"You are mistaken," Chet said. "You planned everything meticulously. But you forgot that the impossible sometimes happens. Every witness against you has died because of accidents. The only one left who might have meant trouble for you is imprisoned, charged with Intelligence with the enemy. You just made one mistake. You tried too hard to be safe. You thought you needed a document and that document would have to stand all tests. You had to prove that Chester Burton himself wrote that letter and, therefore, the letter couldn't be signed by Chester Burton but by the code name, Sagitta. The name Sagitta only three persons know, as you just said. Grandelieu, you and I. I did not write the note. Grandelieu most certainly wouldn't have accused himself of having betrayed me. There is only one left, the third . . . the traitor."

Blois made a sudden move and, before Chet could stop him, flung himself backwards across the bed, reaching under the pillow with a swimmer's vigorous backstroke. From under it with one sure quick grasp he drew a revolver. Chet was upon him instantly and Blois, stumbling back, fell again onto the bed. They wrestled silently, viciously. But Chet had the advantage and eventually secured the revolver.

Oh no, he thought, Blois was not going to murder him for a third time nor could he afford to have Blois shoot himself without any witnesses. Holding Blois at bay with the revolver, he reached out for the telephone.

"Police headquarters."

After he had replaced the receiver he went back to the chair in which he had sat before when he had waited for Blois. He sat quietly, utterly relaxed, only the weapon in his hand turned in Blois's direction revealing his attention.

He had reached his goal. He had accomplished what

he had set out to do. He thought how tragic it must be to die, to die before one had fulfilled the job one had wanted to finish; and a flood of gratitude filled him because he had been allowed to live, at least long enough to eliminate one danger.

How strange life was; each and everything had its price and no one could ever escape paying it . . . just as he was paying for this satisfaction. Nor could anyone gauge himself the price he was willing to pay or the ultimate cost. Hadn't he felt that four years were enough? And now it turned out that in his determination to see justice done he had saved the one man who would ruin all his personal, individual happiness.

He couldn't have one without the other. Pierre Blois's exposure meant a free and safe Robert Grandelieu.

Presently through the night came the shrill scream of wide-open sirens, the screech of brakes, the hammering at the front door. Pierre Blois moved his head, slightly, listening, then sat as before, erect, motionless.

Chet waited until the door opened and he saw three police officers standing on its threshold before he relaxed his vigil. The servant who had admitted the police hurried forward and stood, as if suddenly petrified, staring at his master who remained seated on the end of the narrow bed. Blois made no attempt to speak. Chet noted the bewildered faces of the police officers, their vague, unsure motions. He spoke rapidly in explanation. Then one of the three stepped closer and gradually the other two followed him into the room.

"I am sorry," said the first man. "I am sorry, *mon colonel*. But I must ask you to come with us. I am sure all this is a misunderstanding . . ."

Blois asked for a few minutes of privacy. He rose slowly and, as he passed Chet, their eyes met. Then Chet moved aside. It would be, he thought, just as well. Now, as Blois disappeared into his dressing room, Chet lit a cigarette and, as he held the match, he noticed that his hands were trembling again.

They all heard the door close, the click of the mechanism as the lock of the old-fashioned safe sprang open and then, after a few seconds, the heavy thud of a body falling to the floor. Then silence. Chet stepped forward and flung open the door.

Blois lay on the shining parquet. He was still alive. His arms, stretched on either side of his body, jerked convulsively. At the edge of the carpet was a tiny phial. His eyes opened and remained open. Then he died.

In the ensuing silence the officer in charge ordered one of his men to call for a doctor. He turned to Chet.

"You will have to come with us, captain . . . just a formality." His jaws kept moving after he had spoken, helplessly. There were beads of perspiration on his low forehead and he kept staring at the long, quiet body of the man whom he had revered as a great hero . . . the all-powerful, invulnerable Colonel Blois.

Chet nodded. His throat suddenly went dry, but in his ears the blood began to hum. It was over. All over. From far away a voice seemed to say:

"Apathy. You may belong in one of these categories. You should rest, Paul Mercier . . ."

The breakdown was coming—coming upon him

rapidly, unexpectedly. I'll have to last out the questioning, Chet thought, then . . . oh, never mind . . . never mind. What does it matter? He squared his shoulders.

8

The little lobby of the Hotel Atala was deserted. Behind his desk, the clerk sat asleep. He had loosened his stiff white celluloid collar and Chet could see his pitifully wrinkled old throat with the Adam's apple sticking out, moving gently with his slow tired breath, up and down, up and down as if manipulated by an invisible rubber band.

It seemed cruel to wake him and Chet stood hesitantly gazing at the old man. Then he walked around the desk and picked up one of the cords at the switchboard. He put it into the round opening under Sue's room number, moved the switch and presently he heard her voice.

The voice came soft and sleepily across the wire and shook his heart just for a moment. Then again he felt very tired, and, as his pulse slowed down, he thought: It's all over. That, too, is finished. Everything's over . . . the tension, the strain, my job. Blois is dead and Grandelieu will be released very soon. And Sue? Well, it's all over between Sue and me.

"I just wanted to tell you you don't need to worry any longer. Everything is all right. The charge against Robert will be withdrawn."

He thought he heard her sigh but he couldn't be

quite sure and somehow, too, it did not matter any longer. Then her voice came again, a little higher now with excitement. She said anxiously:

"Chet, Chet! Where are you, for God's sake?"

"Downstairs."

"But come up! Quick."

"It's kind of late," he answered. "It's very late, Sue. I just wanted you to know."

Again there was a pause, then Sue asked gently, "Is anything wrong, Chet? Don't you want to . . ."

"No," he said rudely. No, he didn't want her to thank him. He did not want to see the glow of joy rising in her cheeks, dancing in her eyes, breaking into a smile, pointing up the dimples around her mouth.

"Wait," she said. "Wait, Chet! I'll be down in a moment."

He put down the receiver, flicked down the switch. He did not want to see her.

The clerk was still sleeping, his Adam's apple still agitated; on his open lips lingered a vague smell of onions.

Chet crossed the lobby quickly. He had almost made it when he heard her steps on the last few stairs. She must have run down all the way, not even waiting for the elevator, not risking a delay. He turned around and faced her, shaking his head.

"I am very tired," he said. "I'll call you tomorrow, Sue."

"Oh, Chet," she said, and her hand reached for his. "Oh, Chet." Slowly her eyes filled with tears and she made no attempt to hide them.

"It's all over, Sue," he said. "No need to cry anymore."

She was still looking at him and the tears formed little drops and ran down both of her cheeks. He reached into his pocket and held out a handkerchief.

"Thank you," she said. She was sobbing now. "I am not crying because of Robert . . . I am crying because of you. You and me."

"No need for that, Sue. I am all right."

"Don't you understand?" she said and took another step so that now they were standing very close and he could smell her hair and again a last wild desire to touch her, to run his hand through her curls and let it rest on the nape of her neck, filled him. He moved away a little, holding himself very straight

"Of course, I understand," he said, "and I am not blaming you. That's the way life is. Each of us has to face it his way. No, darling, I am not blaming you for anything. I understand. When they told you I was dead, I *was* dead for you and somehow life went on for you without me. Even when I came back you couldn't bring to life again what you had once felt for me. I understand," he said for a third time, "and I wish you all the happiness in the world. I wish you . . ."

"Chet," she said, her voice suddenly steady, "you don't understand at all. You don't understand that I love you, *you*, not Robert. You don't understand that when you suddenly stood in my room, I . . . it was a shock. I had to behave the way I did. For your sake and mine. To protect us both. To protect what I hoped our future would be. But I was not sure how it would work out, I was not sure to what extent both of us had changed or if we could pick up where we had left off."

He didn't know that he had opened his arms and

that he was holding her tight; then overwhelmingly he felt the warmth of her body, her arms around him.

"I couldn't let you believe the wrong things about Robert just because of our personal situation. I couldn't let Robert be arrested and helpless and maybe . . ." she sighed . . . "just because of you and me. It all ran together, don't you see? I couldn't . . ."

"No," he said slowly. "No, you couldn't, Sue."

And suddenly Chet realized that the girl whom he loved and he had more in common than he had ever bothered to figure out; the strength and conviction to act according to their beliefs, ready to sacrifice their personal happiness, their individual desires, if and when life made it necessary to help and fight for justice and a future which made sense.

The four years which had separated them were no longer of importance; no longer a barrier, but a new foundation because they had both learned that each human was responsible for the other, whoever he might be.

"I love you, Chet," said Sue. "I . . ."

"I never have stopped loving you," he told her.

THE END

Martha Albrand Bibliography
(1914-1981)

Novels:

As by Katrin Holland:
Man spricht über Jacqueline, 1926
Wie macht man das nur ???, 1930
Unterwegs zu Alexander: Ein Liebesroman, 1932
Die silberne Wolke: Ein Roman aus unserer Zeit, 1933
Babett auf Gottes Gnaden, 1934
Das Mädchen, das niemand mochte, 1935
Das Frauenhaus, 1935
Carlotta Torresani, 1938
Einsamer Himmel, 1938
Vierzehn Tage mit Edita, 1939
Helene, 1940
The Obsession of Emmet Booth, 1957

As by Martha Albrand:
No Surrender, 1942
Without Orders, 1943
Endure No Longer, 1944
None Shall Know, 1945
Remembered Anger, 1946
Whispering Hill, 1947
After Midnight, 1948
Wait for the Dawn, 1950
Desperate Moment, 1951
The Hunted Woman, 1953
Nightmare in Copenhagen, 1954; abr mag version as
   "Captive of Fear")
The Mask of Alexander, 1955

The Linden Affair (1956; UK as *The Story That Could Not Be Told;* abr mag version as "Reunion With Terror")
A Day in Monte Carlo, 1959
Meet Me Tonight, 1960; abr mag version as "Return to Terror")
A Call from Austria, 1963
The Door fell Shut, 1966
Rhine Replica, 1969
Manhattan North, 1971
Zurich/AZ 900, 1974
A Taste of Terror, 1976
Final Encore (1978; UK as *Intermission*)

As by Christine Lambert:
The Ball, 1961
A Sudden Woman, 1964

Short Story:

The Other Side of the Moon (*Ladies Home Journal*, May 1947)

Filmography:

Die Nacht der großen Liebe (Germany, 1933)
Talking About Jacqueline (Germany, 1937, based on *Man spricht über Jacqueline*)
Talk About Jacqueline (UK, 1942, based on *Man spricht über Jacqueline*)
Captain Carey, U.S.A. (1950, based on *After Midnight*)
Desperate Moment (UK, 1953, based on *Desperate Moment*)

Martha Albrand was born September 8, 1910 as Heidi Huberta Freybe in Rostock, Germany. Albrand was the name of her Danish great-grandfather. Also known as Katrin Holland, she began her writing career in Europe before coming to the United  States in 1937. Her first American novel was *No Surrender*, which was serialized in *The Saturday Evening Post,* where most of her subsequent novels were first published. Albrand was the author of nearly 40 novels of mystery and suspense, winning the Grand Prix de Littérature Policière International Prize in France for *After Midnight* in 1950. Five movies were made from her novels, including *Captain Carey, U.S.A.* with Alan Ladd. Albrand died at her home in Manhattan on June 24, 1981.

www.ingramcontent.com/pod-product-compliance
Lightning Source LLC
Chambersburg PA
CBHW071945150726
47999CB00001B/310